DAD IN TRAINING

GAIL GAYMER MARTIN

THORNDIKE
CHIVERS

This Large Print edition is published by Thorndike Press, Waterville, Maine, USA and by BBC Audiobooks Ltd, Bath, England.

Thorndike Press, a part of Gale, Cengage Learning.

The text of this Large Print edition is unabridged.

Other aspects of the book may vary from the original edition.

Set in 16 pt. Plantin.

Printed on permanent paper.

LIBRARY OF CONGRESS CATALOGING-IN-PUBLICATION DATA

Martin, Gail Gaymer, 1937–
 Dad in training / by Gail Gaymer Martin.
  p. cm. — (Thorndike Press large print Christian fiction)
 ISBN-13: 978-1-4104-2273-6 (alk. paper)
 ISBN-10: 1-4104-2273-9 (alk. paper)
 1. Special education teachers—Fiction. 2. Human-animal relationships—Fiction. 3. Large type books. I. Title.
 PS3613.A7786D33 2010
 813'.6—dc22   2009037654

BRITISH LIBRARY CATALOGUING-IN-PUBLICATION DATA AVAILABLE

Published in 2010 in the U.S. by arrangement with Harlequin Books S.A. Published in 2010 in the U.K. by arrangement with Harlequin Enterprises II B.V.

U.K. Hardcover: 978 1 408 47772 4 (Chivers Large Print)
U.K. Softcover: 978 1 408 47773 1 (Camden Large Print)

Printed in Mexico
1 2 3 4 5 6 7 14 13 12 11 10

We will be confident when we stand before
the Lord, even if our hearts condemn us.
For God is greater than our hearts,
and he knows everything.

— 1 *John* 3:19–20

In memory of our daughter, Brenda Martin Bailey. Her love of dogs was an inspiration for this series.

ACKNOWLEDGMENTS

Thanks to Amy Johnson — the real Molly Manning, the director of Teacher's Pet in Waterford, who shares Molly's dreams.

Thanks also to Debbie Schutt, director of Oakland Pet Fund, an organization to create a "no more homeless pets" community.

Thanks also to the Michigan Humane Society for adding to my research.

CHAPTER ONE

A long, wet tongue swept across Molly's face. She jerked away and chuckled as she wiped her damp cheek before patting Rowdy's smooth coat. "Is that my goodbye kiss?"

The dog looked at her as if he understood. His eyes reflected love and his mouth formed a Mona Lisa smile.

Molly welcomed the feel of the dog's fur on her palm. In some ways, it reminded her of family — unconditional love, companionship and someone waiting for her when she walked through the door at night. No, it wasn't "Honey, I'm home," but a wagging tail to lift her spirit. That would be much better than the silence that now greeted her.

"He likes you, Miss Manning."

Molly let her hand slip from the dog's fur. "He likes you, too, Adam. He knows how to choose good friends."

Adam nodded, his thick glasses giving him

cartoon eyes. "Dogs have a good mind. They're not like people. They're lovable and willing to forgive."

Her student's amazing insight pinged against her heart as she moved back toward the school's entrance. He had wisdom beyond his years. Knowing Adam's troubles, Molly understood the boy's conviction had deeper meaning for her than most people would register. Forgive? She'd never forgiven herself for what she'd done. She'd ignored her Christian upbringing and morals while in high school, and the shame still crashed down on her and drove her to prove to herself she was worthy of God's blessings.

"Do you have a minute?"

Molly spun around, hearing Rob Dyson's call.

"You want me?" She pointed to herself with her index finger. Her gaze drifted from her principal to the good-looking gentleman beside him.

She held up a finger and turned back to Adam, who'd knelt beside the dog, probably wanting a kiss of his own. "Let's get Rowdy into the van. The bell's going to ring. You don't want to be late for class, do you?" Dumb comment. Adam would love to be late, but she couldn't add that to his other misdemeanors. She glanced over her shoulder at her principal waiting for her in the school entrance foyer.

Adam gave her a teasing smirk. "It's only career day."

She folded her arms across her chest, managing a frown. "But that's important. In a few years, you'll be looking for a job. We all need to know what's possible for us to make our dreams come true." The words smacked her with the truth once again.

The middle-schooler pondered her comment before rising and finally steered Rowdy toward the van that would take him back to the dog shelter. The Labrador retriever climbed into the vehicle, and Adam gave the dog a wave. The boy then ambled back into the school building and down the hallway.

The principal moseyed toward Molly, the handsome stranger following. Before Rob reached her, he eyed his watch. "Is Teacher's Pet done for today?"

She gave him a questioning nod, then lifted her gaze to check on Adam. She wasn't stupid. She needed to make sure the boy turned in the direction of the classrooms and not the cafeteria or a restroom — two of the students' favorite hangouts. When the boy headed in the right direction of his next class, Molly hid a sigh of relief. "Yes. Everyone's accounted for."

"Good." He tilted his head toward the man. "Molly, this is Brent Runyan."

Runyan. The name aroused her interest. So did his amazing eyes. She met his gaze. "Welcome to Montgomery Middle School."

"Thanks," he said, his voice a pleasant rumble. He eyed her a moment before extending his palm.

Molly grasped it, her fingers swallowed in his large hand.

Rob's voice drew her back. "I'm on my way to a meeting, and Brent's doing a career presentation in Joe Edmonds' machine shop. Would you mind showing him the way?"

When she looked into the man's midnight-blue eyes, a warm tingle glided down her arm. She withdrew her hand, trying to control the unfamiliar sensation. Ridiculous. She frowned, managing to get a grip on herself.

Her principal's head drew back. "Look. If you're busy, I'll —"

"No. No. It's fine." She steadied her voice, irritated that the man's presence had thrown her off-kilter. "It's on the way."

"Thanks." Rob grasped Brent's shoulder with a shake. "I'll see you tomorrow at the softball game."

Brent's lips twisted in a crooked smile. "I can't believe you conned me into joining the team."

"We needed a good outfielder," Rob said, shifting his gaze to Molly. "You should see this guy shag a fly ball." He gave Brent's arm another shake. "I hope the class goes well." He took a step backward and glanced at his watch, before lifting his hand in a half-wave.

Molly watched Rob head down the hall-way as she mustered the courage to look at Brent again. "The classroom's this way." She beckoned him to follow. "Not far from the teacher's lounge where I'm headed."

A faint grin twitched on his mouth. "You're a teacher."

"Who did you think I was?"

He shrugged. "Teachers don't look the way they did when I was in school."

As heat rose up her neck, Molly diverted the attention from her face to her feet by picking up her pace. "We'd better get you to class. The bell rang a few minutes ago." She paused and waited for him to catch up. "I received a transfer to Montgomery Middle School three years ago. Before that I taught at the elementary school." The reference led her to one of the questions

15

that struck her when she'd heard his last name. "I had a student there with the last name Runyan. Any relationship, by chance?"

Brent gestured ahead of them. "Is that the classroom? I see a man hanging out the door."

"That's Mr. Edmonds."

He tossed her a look. "I'd better hurry."

He charged forward, apologizing to Joe as he drew closer. He reached the door before her shorter legs could get her there. When she caught up, Joe gave her a nod and beckoned Brent inside before she could introduce them.

Molly ambled away from the classroom, disappointed she couldn't ask him her second question, although he'd never answered her first one about her elementary student, Randy Runyan. Before she'd moved too far away, she heard Brent's voice coming through the open doorway. She paused, hoping to hear what he had to say. She hesitated a moment, enjoying the sound of his lively presentation. It's the way her students made her feel some days.

She loved her misunderstood students and suspected that most of the teachers thought she was a few cookies short of a box. Half of them found her students troublesome. Sure, her kids had special needs, but they were curious, eager and hardworking. The Teacher's Pet class gave them confidence and seemed to add an extra bounce to her step. If only life rejuvenated her the way that class did. Yet always, she struggled with the old longing to do more for dogs and kids.

The classroom became quiet, and Molly quickened her steps toward the teachers' lounge. She'd be mortified if Brent found her still in the hallway.

Brent eyed the wall clock, glad the students had run out of questions. During one of the pauses, his mind had snapped back to Molly. He envisioned her fresh-washed look, not a lot of makeup. Her wheat-colored hair had been tied back in a ponytail except for a few wispy strands that fell across her forehead. He couldn't remember one teacher from his high school days being that cute.

Cute? His chest tightened. Women weren't cute. They were charming or attractive or dowdy or . . . They shouldn't be cute and so appealing. He'd felt horrible, ogling her the way he'd done, but her wholesomeness and bright eyes had grabbed his interest.

And Teacher's Pet. What in the world was that?

He forced his thoughts back to the class

as he dug his hands into his pockets and cleared his throat.

Edmonds scanned the room. "No more questions?"

The students remained silent.

"Then let's thank our guest speaker, Mr. Runyan from Runyan Industrial Tool Corporation. He's given you a good understanding of the kinds of jobs you might find in that line of work."

A couple of kids applauded, and then others followed as Brent nodded in thanks.

Edmonds peered at the wall clock and then tilted his head toward the doorway. "You have a few minutes. Take a break before next period. The teacher's lounge is close." He took a step toward the exit. "Grab a coffee. The stuff's thick as axle grease, but it'll keep you awake."

Axle grease. Brent guessed the guy had background in auto shop, too.

Edmonds joined Brent at the door and gestured to the right. "Make a left at the next hallway. You'll see a sign on the door."

"Thanks," Brent said, regaining his feeling of freedom. He strode in the direction Edmonds had pointed, and near the end of the hall, he saw the sign — Staff Lounge. He grasped the knob, curious what teachers actually did during their planning period.

From stories he'd heard, they did everything but.

When he stepped inside, his curiosity ended. Only one person sat at a round table, flipping through a notebook. Molly.

She looked up and then refocused on her work as she spoke. "Done already?"

"For now."

He eyed her a moment, weighing the tone of her voice. Uncertainty? Distrust? Caution? He couldn't read her.

Brent followed the scent of the stale coffee across the lounge. Though his back was to her, he sensed Molly's eyes boring through him. He grasped a paper cup and poured the liquid into it. He recalled Joe's accurate description, then held the cup beneath a nearby faucet and added a splash of water. While he wanted to face Molly, he drew out the anticipation.

When he swiveled toward her, he found that his suspicion had been correct. Molly watched him. He stood across the room, eyes riveted to hers, asking himself which one would break the connection first.

He took a sip of the acrid drink to control the unexpected sensation of interest. In his distraction, he broke eye contact.

"Have a seat?" Molly's voice sliced through the silence as she motioned toward one of the chairs at her table.

He ambled toward her, his eyes focused on the coffee while he controlled the feeling skittering through his chest. When he settled in the chair, he forced himself to look up.

Molly captured his gaze. "Are you connected with Runyan Industrial Tool Corporation?"

"I am." The response had flown from his mouth, and he nearly spilled his coffee with the unexpected question. She lowered her eyes a moment, giving him a reprieve. Brent took a deep breath.

Molly seemed to ponder his answer. "I've noticed the building on Rochester Road. It's empty, right?"

This time she'd struck a sour chord. "That's temporary."

"Temporary?"

She seemed to scrutinize his response, and Brent became more cautious. That building had become a thorn in his finger.

Molly's expression changed. "I imagine the automotive cutbacks must affect your business." A provoking expression seeped to her face, and he sensed her mind working on something.

The look made Brent edgy. "We make tools for many businesses, not just the automotive industry." He took a sip of the bad coffee, eager to change the subject, and he had the question to do just that. "Rob asked you about a Teacher's Pet class. What's that? Some kind of honor-roll program?" Brent imagined the students falling all over themselves to clean her erasers. "I'll admit I was never one of them." He cringed, admitting way too much. Even worse, he was flirting, and he didn't realize he knew how.

She cocked her head. "Far from it."

His head jerked back. "What do you mean?"

She grinned for the first time since he'd entered the room. "Be assured it's not a group of favorite students cleaning chalkboards for extra credit."

Her expression made him smile. "No?" But if it were, he might not mind belonging to the group. His heart gave a thump. The dangerous thought had jumped into his mind without warning. Instinctively, he blinked. "So what is —" The last word vanished beneath a loud *brrring.*

"The bell," she said, snapping closed her notebook and rising from her chair. "I have to get to my classroom and unlock the door. My students get in trouble if I don't."

She breezed past him, leaving his half question unanswered.

He closed his mouth, recalling that the bell also summoned him to the next career presentation. Not wanting to be late again, Brent strode to the sink, poured out the potent coffee, and tossed the cup into the trash. Teacher's pet? The question settled in his mind, and he speculated what it might be like to be one.

Molly pulled into Stephanie Wright's drive-way and hit two short blasts on the horn to signal she'd stopped by. With Steph, she never felt as if she needed to call ahead, although she never stopped anywhere else without calling — even her folks. Her chest clutched, realizing that that was weird. She had great parents, but those bad teen years had ruined her dreams of being a veterinar-ian and her reputation had put a wedge between her and them. The wedge was hers. Her parents had forgiven her long ago.

Molly slammed the lid on her memories and pushed opened the car door to the sound of yipping and a couple of solid woofs from inside the house. The dining room curtain shifted as she headed toward the porch. She grinned when her friend's border collie's nose pressed against the pane. Steph's smile soon appeared, and she sent Molly a wave.

As Molly bounded up the porch steps, the door opened, and Steph pushed the screen door wider to allow her entrance while managing to keep three dogs from escaping.

"Hello, Fred." Molly scratched her friend's border collie behind the ears and then gave the terrier's fur a fluff and nuzzled her cheek against the Airedale's head. "Who do we have here?"

"Sam, and this one's Trixie." Steph pointed to the terrier. "Their owners aren't here yet." She glanced at her watch. "They should be coming soon. I have to leave for my other job." She lifted her head, her expression growing curious. "You're grinning." She tapped her index finger against her cheek. "Let me see. I'm guessing most of your kids were absent today."

Molly smiled at Steph's banter. "Sorry to disappoint you, but they were all there." She arched one eyebrow. "But you'll never guess what happened."

"You got a raise?"

"I don't look *that* happy." With the three dogs tangling around her feet, Molly made her way into the living room, tossed her handbag onto a side table, and plopped into an easy chair. "I met someone."

That comment caught Steph's attention,

23

and a Cheshire cat grin spread across her face. "You mean . . . Mr. Right?"

Air shot from Molly's lungs. "No. Never." Her voice sounded like someone evading the truth.

Steph gave her a questioning look.

"Just kidding," she said, hoping to undo the suspicion she'd caused. "I met Brent Runyan."

Steph's hand flew to her heart. "Wow! Brent Runyan. I'm impressed." Her hand dropped to her side as she settled onto the sofa. "I need a seat so I can contain myself." She leaned forward, emphasizing the Cheshire grin. "Who in the world is Brent Runyan?"

Molly felt her jaw sag as she shook her head at Steph's antics. "You've heard of Runyan Industrial Tool Corporation. The building on Rochester Road."

Steph looked blank.

Molly's arms lifted in a helpless gesture and then dropped to her side. "The empty building on Rochester Road. I told you about it."

Finally recognition sprouted on Steph's face. "Is he the owner?"

"Brent Runyan. Runyan Industrial Tool Corporation. What do you think?"

Steph lifted a shoulder. "Okay, so I'm a

little brain dead. I spent my day with five barking dogs."

Hearing the word *dogs,* all three animals skittered to Steph's side. "Get lost," she said, waving her hand at them before refocusing on Molly.

"You're as bad as some of my students. 'Down' is all you need to say and then show them. They'll catch on."

Steph rolled her eyes. "Let's talk about this Runyan character."

Molly had a better description than character. *Good-looking* worked for her. Steph's look bored through her, and Molly knew she'd better get on with it. "Okay, I suppose, I can't expect you to remember every empty building I've given a longing look."

"You've eyed a ton of them."

Images flashed through Molly's mind — empty office buildings, industrial businesses, grocery stores. She'd never found one that would work as perfectly as the Runyan building, but the cost was prohibitive. Most buildings were.

"Did you ask this Runyan guy about the building?"

Steph's voice dragged her from her ruminations, and she sank against the cushion. "Not really. When I mentioned it was empty, he said, 'That's temporary.' I question that, though. How long has it been since I've had my eye on that building?"

"It's your guess." Steph unfolded herself from the chair and glanced out the window. "I thought I heard a car."

Molly understood. "I know you have to leave for work."

Steph gave a faint nod and ambled back toward her chair. "I have to wait for the owners to get here and pick up their pooches." She leaned her head against the chair back. "I wish I could get one full-time job instead of two part-times, but as long as I want to do doggie day care, this is it."

"You need a building, Steph, and do this job on a grander scale."

Steph lifted her head. "You're optimistic."

"When I find a building, you could make a living with the dogs then. No need for a second job. It'll work." Molly's chest tightened, thinking of Steph's dream and then her own. "I know your neighbors get upset when the dogs are noisy."

Steph's face mirrored her concern. "You and I are like kids waiting for a dream to happen. When will we grow up?" She sat again and closed her eyes. "That's not fair. You have a real job. When will I grow up?"

"We're both grown up, but we care about dogs. I enjoy teaching, but if I could have a dog shelter, that would be my ultimate dream. Then I could run other Teacher's Pet programs there, and you could use some space for your day care. It would be wonderful. Perfect." Molly leaned forward, wishing she had a house instead of a condo. Then she could have a dog of her own. "You know, I believe God has plans, and I'm hoping having a shelter is His plan for me . . . eventually. I have to learn patience."

"Patience." Steph's head made a slight nod.

They sat in silence as Molly pictured her long-awaited dream and assumed Steph was doing the same. Money. That's what they needed. Both of them. "I'd better let you get ready for work." She rose and moved toward her handbag.

Steph stood, too. "What will you do now?"

Molly hung the bag on her shoulder. "About what?"

"The building. Is this Runyan guy someone you'll see again? Aren't you going to pursue it?"

"Yes. I just have to figure out how." Molly adjusted her shoulder strap and then straightened as her mind sparked an idea. "Hold on. Are you working tomorrow night?"

"I'm not off until Friday."

"I'll go alone then." Disappointed, she made her way toward the door.

"Go? Go where?"

"To the softball game. My principal knows Brent Runyan. They're on a team together, and they play tomorrow night."

"Isn't that a little obvious?"

"I'll see what I can find out from Rob tomorrow. I could go and cheer them on."

Steph pressed her palm to her cheek, her eyes widening. "You can't be serious."

"I am serious. Why not? If I went with someone, I wouldn't look so suspect, but it's worth it. I'll see him again, and maybe we'll talk."

Steph stared at her with an "I can't believe you'd do this" expression.

"Okay, so it's probably a dumb plan." Molly grasped the strap of her shoulder bag. "What else can I do? I need to find out what he means by 'temporary' without making it a big deal."

Steph shifted closer, her mouth curved in one of her taunting looks. "Are you sure it's just the building you're interested in?"

Molly jammed her fists against her hips and scowled. "Yes, I'm sure."

A look of temporary defeat settled on Steph's face. "Having money for a building would make a difference."

"Money talks, but when money isn't available, I talk."

Steph leaned down and wrapped her arm around Molly's shoulders. "Poor guy. He doesn't know what he's in for." She gave Molly a hug.

Molly hugged her back and then opened the front door. One thing she appreciated was a good friend who really knew her. Steph understood, and she was right. Poor Brent Runyan wouldn't know what hit him.

She sent Steph one of her Cheshire cat grins and then stepped outside and closed the door, but Molly didn't move. Something had hit her, too. Something that jarred her pulse with excitement and with dread. She rubbed her temple and headed to her car.

The building had to be her focus and not Brent Runyan and his gorgeous eyes. Romantic notions weren't an option. As a Christian woman, she'd set the atonement for her mistakes.

The Runyan building settled in her thoughts. She wanted that empty building. It was perfect, but before she turned the key in the ignition, the building faded behind a pair of midnight-blue eyes.

CHAPTER TWO

Brent stood in left field and waited for the next batter in the lineup. The other team had two men on base and a good hitter at bat. Brent knew he had to concentrate. With one out and the game separated by one run, this was it. One slip-up and they could lose the game.

The sun had lowered in the sky, and a direct glare hit Brent in the eyes. He adjusted his cap, dug his fist into the mitt, and squinted into the bleachers. A glint of gold caught his attention, and his jaw dropped. Molly. What was she doing —

A sharp crack and cheers from the crowd jarred his senses. Instinctively his eyes shifted as the ball blasted toward him. He raced backward, angry at himself for being distracted, then lifted his arm and felt the ball smash into his glove. He drew back and shot the ball, head high, to the catcher. The runner on third slid toward home base, but the catcher caught the ball and tagged him. Out.

Brent's heart jolted. He'd been saved from a mishap, and they'd won the game. He tossed his glove in the air and ran toward his teammates, as they thumped each other on the back. Someone grasped him in a bear hug and others followed.

"Great game, Brent."

"Good save."

Pure luck. He smiled and nodded, unwilling to admit he'd almost lost the game with his foolish distraction. He looked into the stands, but the golden hair had vanished. His imagination wasn't that creative. He knew it was Molly, but what in the world was she doing there?

"Great job," Rob said, wrapping an arm around his shoulder before pummeling his back with the flat of his hand. "Let's celebrate. Want to stop for a drink?"

"How about a sandwich and some coffee? I missed dinner."

"That works for me." Rob pulled out a handkerchief and wiped sweat from his face. "This is only May. I hate to think of the heat this summer."

Brent nodded without really listening. Ahead of them, Molly waited near the stands alone, holding a soft-drink cup.

31

Rob faltered beside him and came to a halt. "Molly? What are you doing here?"

Just the question Brent had on his mind. He waited for her answer.

She smiled and shrugged. "I heard you mention softball yesterday and thought I'd stop by and watch. You know, cheer on my favorite principal."

Rob chuckled. "Am I getting a little apple-polishing here?" He threw his head back and laughed. "We're heading out to pick up a bite. Want to join us?"

Brent watched her face light up as her gaze drifted toward him.

Her eyes grazed his. "Would you mind?"

He wasn't sure if the question was directed to him or Rob, so he didn't respond. If he'd answered, she would have been able to tell he minded. She addled him, and he couldn't control his attraction. On top of that, she asked too many questions, questions that dug into sensitive issues. Brent played in today's game to get away from the tension. Here she was with her innocent face digging up problems he preferred buried.

Rob's voice cut into his thoughts. "Mind? Not at all, I invited you."

She didn't shift her gaze from his, and an uneasy feeling crawled up Brent's back. His reservation got lost in her dazzling green-flecked hazel eyes. "Where are we going?" He turned his question to Rob.

"How about National Coney Island? It's not far. North on Dixie Highway." He shifted from Brent to Molly. "Sound okay?"

Molly shrugged. "It's fine with me."

If he could only think of a good reason to — no, he couldn't. If he backed out, Rob would make a big deal out of it and want to know why. He tossed the possibility around in his mind, but when he opened his mouth, he heard himself agree.

Rob clapped his palms together. "Great. Let's go. I need something cold to drink." He mimed a swig from an imaginary bottle.

Brent watched him lead the way with Molly at his side, flustered by her slender figure, the ponytail and her flawless skin. She bounced along with each step while he trudged behind her, his shoulders tensing with anticipation, and his heart jigging faster than his plodding feet. He despised the absurd feeling.

Molly climbed into a red SUV while he settled into his ebony sports car. She belonged in something flashy and fun like a sports car. He belonged . . . where? Something solid, he supposed, but definitely not red. Black fit him better.

He sank into the leather seats, questioning

his sanity and shaking his head as if the motion could knock some sense into him. He didn't get involved with women. He didn't have time, and his life was too complicated already.

Molly watched the dark sports car flash past her, raising dust from the parking lot. She gripped the steering wheel, wondering if she was making a mistake. Brent didn't seem eager for her company, although why should he? Maybe if he got to know her better, he'd recognize her sincerity about her work.

Her back rigid with purpose, Molly drove away from the park and headed north on Dixie Highway. All she'd wanted to do is get to know more about his empty building. She winced, knowing that that was only part of the truth.

How could she introduce the subject of his building during their conversation? With her determination, she would make a blue-ribbon effort.

Sunlight beat against her arm and glinted in her eye, and she adjusted the visor. She'd felt as sunny as the sky while she watched the game, hoping she'd have a chance to talk with Brent, but now her hope darkened like a storm cloud. Brent could easily evade her questions again.

Maybe she'd read more into things than there was. She remembered Adam's comment the day before. The boy had said dogs weren't like people. They sure weren't. Dogs were honest. That's one of the things she loved about them. No pretenses. They let her know immediately how they felt about her. They either wagged their tail and licked her hand or bared their teeth. She never had to guess with a dog.

With her pretext of cheering on the game, she'd been deceiving. Brent was no different. She closed her muddled thoughts and turned into the restaurant parking lot. Guessing got her nowhere. Brent and Rob stood outside the restaurant entrance waiting for her. Molly parked and headed toward reality.

Inside, the scent of onions and chili powder mingled in the air. The hostess guided them to a booth, and Rob slipped in one side, sitting in the middle of the bench, so she slid to the wall on the other side, making room for Brent.

Rather than joining them, Brent stood beside the table, eyeing the seating arrangement. Molly's stomach knotted, waiting for him to ask Rob to move over. She struggled to hold back her mortification.

Instead Brent gestured toward the back of

the dining room. "I need to wash my hands." Without pause, he turned and walked away.

Molly pulled her gaze from his retreating back.

Rob leaned against the seat back. "You surprised me today."

"I did?" She hoped her voice sounded normal.

"Seeing you in the bleachers. Thanks for coming. I always hope a few of the staff will show up, but it's rare."

"I'm glad I came." She had to restrain her hope. "You said I should see Brent shag a ball, so I did."

He chuckled. "He's good, isn't he? And we won. Maybe you're our lucky charm."

She forced a grin, her ulterior motive intensifying her guilty conscience.

Grateful for the distraction, Molly relaxed when the waitress arrived with the menus. Rob grasped them and handed two to Molly and placed one in front of himself.

The woman lifted her pad. "Would you like something to drink?"

"Unsweetened iced tea with lemon," Molly said without looking at the menu.

Rob eyed the choices. "I'll have a soda." He patted the extra menu. "I'm not sure what he'll have." He gestured in the direction Brent had headed, then tilted his head. "Here he comes. You can ask him yourself."

The waitress walked away, pausing to talk with Brent. When he returned to the table, Brent peered at the two booth benches, obviously noting that Rob was sitting close to the edge. He grasped the menu from the table and slid into the seat next to Molly.

"I'll only be a minute," Rob said, rising from his seat and striding toward the back.

Brent perused the meal choices without responding.

Drawing in the fresh fragrance of soap that mingled with the scent of chili dogs, Molly opened the menu and studied it before placing it back on the table. "Are you upset about something?"

In slow motion, Brent lowered his menu, one eye narrowed as if he were scrutinizing her comment. "Why?"

"I don't know why. You just seem tense."

"I can't decide what to order."

She knew it was more than that. She stopped her questions and refocused on the entrée choices.

As she did, Brent shifted on the bench and looked at her.

His eyes glinted as an unbelievable sensation slid along her chest. "What?" The question shot from her mouth.

He leaned his shoulder against the booth cushion and arched a brow. "Since I have you captive —" he motioned to her pinned beside him "— how about answering my question?"

"Your question?" Her mind flashed over their conversation. "You mean why I thought you looked upset?"

"No." A grin stole to his face. "Yesterday I asked you about Teacher's Pet."

"Oh, that question." The unexpected discussion of her program thrilled her. She chuckled. "It's a program I developed for some of the learning-disabled students at the school. I had the idea of putting dog training and student training together."

"Dogs? In school?"

His dubious tone caused her to falter a moment before she responded. "And kids."

He looked confused, and she paused, taking the opportunity to let her gaze sweep across his broad shoulders before she shifted her eyes to his bare ring finger resting on the table. Attractive. Really good-looking, even a little witty, but his tone concerned her. "Don't you like animals?"

"Too much work. They make messes and tear up things. I don't want to be hur—" He blinked, then continued, "To waste time caring for pets. I have enough going on in my life."

Her spirit sank, and a sound in his voice made her sad. She couldn't stop herself from asking: "Have you ever owned a pet?"

She felt him stiffen beside her, and she knew for certain she should have followed her good sense and not pushed the subject.

"Once. It's just too much for me."

Too much what? This time her intelligence halted her next question. "The program helps the students, too. I hope you like kids."

He drew in a deep breath. "I do."

Despite what he'd said, she'd struck a sour note with him in some way. Something bothered him. A lot. "These are special-needs students, remember?"

He rested an elbow on the table and lowered his chin. "How does the program work?"

Interest flashed in his eyes, and Molly took advantage of the opportunity. Once he understood her program, he might realize why she wanted his building. Molly pulled back her shoulders. "Students who often experience failure feel inadequate and can become discipline problems. They don't respect themselves, so they don't respect others. My idea has been to see what happens when kids who have certain learning disabilities work with dogs."

A questioning look rose to his face. "Is this program for kids of all ages?"

"Yes. School-age kids." His curiosity drove her forward. "This technique has even been used with autistic children of all ages. As students teach the dogs to respond correctly to single-word commands — you know, words like *sit, stay, off, down* and *come* — they are also learning behavior modification and gaining skills."

Brent's mouth pulled at one edge. "You mean the kids learn to sit, stay and come."

A frustrated breath slipped from her. "No."

"Just teasing," he said, wiping the toying look from his face.

"When the students realize they've succeeded in teaching the dog something, they feel successful, too. It's amazing."

"You really believe in this system, don't you?"

"I do." She gave an emphatic nod. "It works. They learn pride, and they learn how good behavior is rewarded just like the dogs are rewarded."

"How are they rewarded?"

The waitress appeared beside them with their drinks. "Sorry. We have a crowd tonight." She set the drinks on the table and asked for their orders. Brent ordered a

Coney Special, and Molly decided on a tossed salad rather than the large fries he'd ordered.

Brent gave a toss of his head. "See the guy standing over there? Ask him what he wants. He owns the other drink."

The waitress looked over her shoulder, nodded and headed for Rob, leaving them alone again.

Molly didn't want to stop their conversation now and answered his last question. "We reward the dogs with bits of dry dog food each time they follow their rules."

His eyes crinkled with his grin. "I meant, how do you reward the students?"

"Oh." She flashed him a helpless look. "The kids are rewarded by gaining respect and learning that they can accomplish something."

"And that works? Their behavior changes."

His tone had softened, and the new interest restored her hope. "Yes, and best of all, the students feel loved. Everyone needs to know they're loved. Animals and people. Dogs feel loved with all the attention they receive, and the kids experience love by the dogs' tail-wagging and eagerness to be with them. It's a win-win situation."

He became thoughtful. Molly noticed a dark look on his face. She let well enough alone, happy they'd actually had a real conversation.

"Teacher's Pet means a lot to you." He gave her a tender smile.

"Yes, it does. It not only helps troubled kids, but it benefits dogs. They are trained and can become family pets rather than be put to sleep."

She'd made a connection. Molly closed her eyes, trying to be succinct. "Think about it. Dogs are loyal. If they love you, they love with their whole heart. They'd give their life for you. You can trust them. Their love is faithful."

Brent shifted in his seat, as if he were trying to make the bench longer to distance himself from her. After a period of silence that seemed an eternity to Molly, he lifted his head and looked into her eyes. "You're right."

"I am?"

"Dogs have unconditional love."

His comment jolted her. He'd agreed with her, and she hadn't expected it at all.

Before any more could be said, Rob slipped onto the bench and eyed them. "Sorry. A couple guys from the team stopped me. One wanted to know who you are." He gave Molly a wink. "I told him you're a softball fan." He grabbed his drink and took a lengthy swallow, then wagged his hand from Brent to her. "What's up?"

Rob's comment hadn't sat well with Molly. Now she feared her principal wondered if she were looking for brownie points or flirting. "I was telling Brent about Teacher's Pet."

"It's a great class." Rob veered his gaze toward Brent with a prideful expression. "The county education department thinks so, too. They wouldn't toss their money away for nothing."

Brent gave an agreeing nod before the conversation shifted to softball. Molly let her mind wander, trying to make sense out of Brent's hot-and-cold manner. She didn't take it personally, but she knew she'd triggered a memory or a problem in his life that he couldn't handle well. He'd fade out when she talked about pets and then turned 180 degrees with his curiosity about her program.

Molly listened to the men as they relived the game plays, wishing Rob had stayed with his other friends.

Finally Rob seemed to notice Molly had been shut out of the conversation, and he turned his focus to her. "I told you Brent was a good outfielder, didn't I?"

"You mentioned it."

"Did you see him shoot the ball to home plate? Batter out. We win." Rob reached over the table with a fist and gave Brent's shoulder a playful poke.

"Very nice," she said, feeling Brent's arm brush against hers.

Brent fiddled with his napkin and took a sip of his soft drink.

Their silence ended when the waitress delivered their orders. After the woman walked away, everyone focused on their meals. Molly sent up a silent blessing for the food and for wisdom. Before she took a bite, she had an idea. Trying to talk to Brent about dogs or his property wouldn't be fruitful today. She'd missed the chance with Rob's reappearance. She swallowed a hunk of lettuce and listened to the silence as long as she could before her mind veered back to the building she'd been interested in for so long.

She had her foot in the door, and she didn't plan on having it closed now. Though she needed to move slowly, Molly had no thought of giving up. She believed in providence, and she couldn't believe that God would guide two people to meet, as she and Brent had done, without a purpose. Everything had a reason, and she would have to pray God's purpose and hers were the same.

44

■ ■ ■ ■

Brent leaned back in his office chair and pondered the prior evening when Molly had finagled her way into his life. Her face hung in his thoughts, and as close as he was to her in the booth, he realized her beauty was real — definitely not artificial. He cupped his hands against the back of his neck and squeezed the taut muscles and then dropped his arms to his desk, happy he'd never see her again.

The thought startled him. As much as her digging into his life and his emotions bothered him, the idea of never seeing her again left him empty. Since they'd met, she'd added a little spark to his boring life. She made him feel different — more alive. She added new bumps to his rutted life — running the family business, playing softball and trying to entertain Randy on weekends. He didn't need anyone adding new potholes.

Molly wanted her questions answered and she wasn't a quitter. He saw it in her eyes, as if she looked right through his body into his heart. No man wanted anyone, let alone a woman with perfect skin and bright eyes, to strip him of his privacy. She couldn't fool him. She wanted something.

But what?

He molded his palms around the base of his neck again and leaned back in his chair while he stared at the ceiling. His thoughts drifted to their earlier conversations. He plowed through what he could recall. She talked about dogs. Obviously they were the focus of her life, even more perhaps than her students. But what about a man in her life? A weight fell on Brent's shoulders, then faded. She had to be single.

One thing he knew for sure. She had guts. She'd appeared at the ball game with her feeble story of supporting Rob, but that didn't seem the real reason. She and Rob hadn't talked much, like friends would. She had an ulterior motive, but he was smart. Molly couldn't hide the truth from him for long.

The truth. What had he and Molly talked about beside dogs? He shuffled their past conversations through his mind. She'd asked about Randy, but the conversation had been interrupted, and he'd never answered.

Would anyone get through to the boy? At eleven he was too withdrawn, too silent, too . . . too much heartache. Even therapy hadn't made a difference in the boy's life.

A light turned on in Brent's mind. The empty building. *"I've noticed the building on Rochester Road. It's empty, right?"* That's what she'd said. Why would she care about an unoccupied building? He pondered the question a moment, feeling like Sherlock Holmes, trying to solve "The Case of the Empty Building." And his nemesis was a pretty young woman with golden hair and flawless skin.

"Something interesting up there?"

Brent's seat catapulted forward as he opened his eyes. "Frank." He struggled to reformat his mind. He motioned to his business manager. "Come in. I wanted to talk with you anyway." He leaned forward and rested his elbow on the desk. "Any bites on the Rochester Road property?"

Frank shook his head. "Not even a nibble."

"Nothing?" Taxes and wasted resources became dollar signs. "What's your thought?"

Frank slipped into a chair and shook his head. "Keep trying. With the economy, nothing's selling. We're stuck. Who knows how long?"

Brent pinched his lip. "I need to get over there and take a look. I mean look at it creatively. Entrepreneurs are buying properties and turning them into apartments and lofts. Are we reaching that market?"

"Are you serious?" He shrugged. "The location's not in the thick of things like Royal Oak. Builders turn gas stations into boutiques and office buildings into condos in that area, but here, it's not likely. In Royal Oak, they rent those things to students at Oakland Community College and the young businessmen and women who want to be near boutiques and cafés, and it's close to the freeway. Our building isn't near anything."

"I'll still take a look. We need to be creative. If we can't see value in the building, no one else will, either."

"You're the boss."

Brent nodded. "I know." And he liked it that way. He liked being independent and making decisions without someone else's pressure. Since his father had backed off and let Brent run the company — finally — Brent wanted to keep it that way.

"And since you are the boss —" Frank leaned forward in the chair and grinned "— here's why I stopped in. We're having an odd problem with one of the machines. Can we talk a minute?"

Since Molly had plopped into Brent's mind and seemed to stay there, he welcomed business issues. Anything to distract him. "Sure, I can give you more than a minute. Take an hour."

Frank's eyebrows raised, then he smiled, assuming that he was teasing, Brent guessed.

But he wasn't.

Molly locked her condo door, hurried out to Steph's car, and slipped inside. Though Fred greeted her with a welcoming tail wag, Steph's welcome wasn't as warm.

"I don't get this," Steph said, backing from the driveway. "Why did you ask me to bring the dog, and what am I doing?"

"I explained it to you on the phone. Fred's our cover."

Steph's forehead looked like a washboard. "Our what?"

"Cover. Two women walking a dog. It looks innocent."

Steph's eyes widened. "I hope so. I'm not planning to be guilty of anything."

"We're not guilty. Not at all, but if anyone spots us looking around, they won't be as suspicious with Fred. You know how dogs like to sniff things." Molly threw her back against the seat cushion. "I've wanted to snoop around that empty building for so long, and I wasn't motivated because it all seemed so out of reach. But Steph, I'm telling you, meeting Brent Runyan means something."

"What?"

"I don't know, but it does." She smacked her chest with her palm. "I feel it in here."

"Well, I'm feeling this plan in the pit of my stomach, and I don't like it."

Molly reached over and patted Steph's hand that gripped the steering wheel. "I'm not trying to drag you into this, but I need an opinion and some creative ideas. This could benefit you as much as me."

"You mean we'll keep each other company in jail?"

"Come on, it's not that bad." Was it? She'd begun acting like a stalker — not stalking a person but a building.

"Tell me again why you think you can use this building without paying rent or buying it." Steph's voice picked up an edge of sarcasm.

"It'll be like a donation. A tax write-off for the company."

"And you think this will happen because you read a newspaper article about a couple of women who had a building donated to them?"

"Yes. I told you about it. If it happens once, it can happen again. It's a great idea and not that off-the-wall." Molly clasped her fingers in her lap, feeling Fred's hot breath near her hair. She wished she could help Steph train her dog, but sometimes Steph was as stubborn as the Alaskan husky Molly had tried to train. The dog acted deaf and blind to her commands and her hand signals, but when she'd been ready to give up, the dog finally followed her direction. Persistence and patience. That's what she needed with Steph. "You really can teach an old dog new tricks."

Steph's nose wrinkled. "What?"

"You know what I mean," she said, aware she'd spoken her thoughts aloud. Along with the thought, Molly's mind shot to Brent. He could change, too, if he really understood what she needed and how worthwhile the program was for kids. "Brent says he doesn't like animals, but he could change."

"I don't know, Molly. I think you're getting in too deep, and you're way too optimistic."

Getting in too deep, huh? She wanted what she wanted, and she didn't think that was too much to ask. But Brent didn't get it. Only two days ago they were strangers. Today he'd become the center of her purpose. And he intrigued her. Amid his wavering responses, a tenderness peeked through his eyes. He'd apologized to her in his own way, more than once. Something kept him from opening up to people. She even noticed his restraint with Rob. If he could step beyond his self-imposed barricade, she might have a chance with her idea.

Molly faced the unexpected truth. She liked Brent, and though she guessed he wasn't much older than she, he seemed a man too weighted down for his years. At thirty, she felt young at heart. Despite their differences, her unwanted thoughts about him didn't seem to budge.

"I'm sorry I hurt your feelings."

Steph's voice broke her contemplation. "You didn't. I'm just thinking. You might be right, but I'm looking for a miracle, and I know the Lord can provide one, if it's His will."

"Maybe it's not all optimism. I know you believe, and how do we ever know if it's the Lord talking to us if we don't take a chance?"

Molly's tension eased. "Thanks. I'm glad you understand."

"I'm trying to." Steph grinned at her. "Should I park in front of the building?" She cocked her head toward the industrial building ahead of them.

"No. Go up a couple of blocks and around

the corner. Then we're really walking Fred."

As Steph passed the Runyan building, something new captured Molly's interest: a large sign in the front window. So that was it. Her heart pressed against her lungs. "It's for sale, Steph. That's what Brent meant about it being empty only temporarily."

"But it's not sold."

A sigh burst from her chest. "There's no sign that says sold, but who knows." Her spirit sank even deeper. "I don't know what I'm doing here now."

Steph turned down a side street and stopped. "We're here. We might as well take a look."

Molly climbed out, opened the backseat door and grasped Fred's leash. "Come on, big guy. Let's go for a walk." As the last word hit the air, Fred bounded from the car and jerked Molly forward with such force she nearly tripped on the curb. She tugged the leash, shortened it and drew the dog to her side. "Heel."

Steph came around the car toward them. "He likes to run."

"When he's on a leash, he should learn to walk."

Steph dug her hands into her jeans pockets and didn't utter a sound.

Molly let it drop and kept a tight rein on

Fred. Into the second block, Fred trotted along beside her without tension, and Molly relaxed the leash, taking a chance. When the dog moved ahead and looked over his shoulder at her, Molly repeated the "heel" command. She grinned when Fred slowed and stayed beside her.

She needed to give Fred nibbles for being good, but her pockets were empty. The word *empty* squeezed her heart. Ahead she could see the unoccupied building. If she only had something to offer Brent, anything to tempt him to let her use the building, her worries would be over. Something other than money. If he had a dog, she could train it or —

"I know you're upset with me." Steph's voice broke their silence.

"I'm not. I'm just thinking about this property and dreaming." She linked her arm with her friend's. "I appreciate your being here. I hope you know that."

Steph's pace quickened. "That's fine, but let's get this over with. You promised to buy me dinner."

She had promised a meal. She needed Steph for moral support and Fred for the walk around the vacated building. She whispered a little prayer as she reached the building and stopped. "I don't remember the security fence." Fred hesitated beside her, sniffing the ground.

Steph moved ahead. "Let's try the other side. Maybe there are windows along the street."

Pausing beside the Realtor sign, Molly pulled a pencil from her purse, located an old receipt and jotted down the Realtor's telephone number. "Hold up." She beckoned to Steph. "I want to look at the gate." She walked closer and touched it. "It's not locked."

Steph drew closer. "What if it's on an alarm system? One of those silent ones where the police show up and drag us off to the pokey."

"You've watched too many movies." She pushed the gate, and it swung back.

Fred lunged forward and bounded onto the property with Molly clinging to the leash. "Heel." She tightened the leash and shortened it.

The dog lurched and then stepped to her side. Molly wanted to gloat at Steph, but right now, she had other things on her mind. She headed toward the first window and brushed away the grime. "It looks like office space."

Steph joined her, shielding the glare from the glass and peeked inside. "Probably is."

Molly hurried ahead, instinctively tightening her hold on Fred, who seemed to be catching on. Facing the next window, Molly leaned her forehead against the glass and peered. "Here we go." She stepped back. "What do you think?"

Steph took Molly's place and squinted through the pane. "It's a huge area. I can picture dog pens and an area for indoor playtime when it's raining."

Molly circled around looking at the open space. "And this side yard could be fenced for a dog run and still have room for parking."

Steph moved away from the window and stood beside her. "It could work nicely, but Molly, no one's going to give you this space for nothing."

"A small amount. Very small. Why not? It happened for those women in the newspaper."

Steph snorted. "Right."

"One more window." Molly motioned ahead and gave more leash to Fred as she settled in front of the next window. She rubbed the gray smudge from the pane and cupped the light from her eyes as she leaned forward.

"Oh, no." She jerked away, tripping over Fred.

"What is it? A body?" Steph yelled.

"Yes, but he's moving, and I'm sure he saw me."

"Security guard?"

"No." Molly felt her legs weaken. "Brent Runyan."

CHAPTER THREE

Brent stumbled backward. His imagination had played tricks on him. Molly had been on his mind continually, and now he'd even imagined seeing her through the window. He grasped control of his senses and headed for the door. Though it couldn't be Molly, he wanted to find out who was outside — hopefully someone interested in the property.

He strode across the cement floor stained with years of use and swung open the door. A black-and-white dog bounded toward him, its leash trailing in the dirt. He jumped back to avoid an attack, but the door had closed behind him, and he stumbled against the building, flinging his hand forward to ward off the animal. The dog slid to a halt, its pink tongue thrashing his outstretched palm.

Once he'd grasped the dog's collar, Brent looked toward the gate standing ajar. He cupped his mouth in his hands. "Hello. You left your dog."

No one responded.

He looked down, feeling a piece of metal press against his fingers and spotted the license along with an ID tag. He bent down to read it, and to his surprise, the dog sat at his heel. Before he could twist the tag around, a shadow fell at his feet. When he lifted his gaze, two women faced him, one a stranger.

"Molly?" He searched her flushed face, hoping to make sense of this new intrusion but grateful that seeing her from inside hadn't been a crazy apparition. "Are you following me?"

Her hand flew to her chest as her eyes widened. "No. I was — I was walking the dog."

"You were walking the dog . . . here?" He flung his arm toward the side yard of the factory.

The woman he didn't know bent down and clapped her hands. "Fred, come here."

"Whose dog is this anyway?" He looked from Molly's guilty face to the stranger.

The woman tilted her head upward. "He's mine."

"And you are?"

"Molly's friend. Stephanie Wright."

As Molly's dazed look faded, Brent suspected she was trying to come up with an excuse, probably an explanation that he wouldn't believe anyway. That sweet face was guilty of something, the innocent face with a telltale smudge on her forehead. "Now I'm curious, Molly. Why not walk your own dog?"

Her angelic expression melted. "I don't own a dog."

He stepped backward. "You mean to tell me a woman who works with dogs and loves them doesn't own one. Why?"

"I live in a condo, and pets aren't allowed."

"So here you are walking your friend's dog." He scratched his head. "But why are you walking him here?"

When Brent saw Molly's expression, he realized he'd sounded too sharp.

"I'm not looking for a place to walk a dog."

Though totally confused, he managed a grin. "What are you doing then?"

She paused and pursed her well-shaped lips. "It's true we were walking the dog, but I need to be honest."

Brent chuckled. "Great start."

"Fred was a ploy to . . . to waylay suspicion."

60

Her guileless expression made him want to laugh, but he saw how serious she was and controlled himself. "Suspicion?"

"We were worried someone would see us and call the police," Stephanie said.

Molly shot her a frown. "We didn't mean to trespass. I just wanted to look inside your building."

His mind swirled with hypotheses. "You have a buyer for this property?"

Her hands dropped to her sides, and he couldn't stop his grin when the dog gave her fingers a broad swipe.

"Not exactly." She wiped her hand on her pantleg.

The vague conversation reminded him of trying to communicate with Randy. The boy's reclusive behavior worried him beyond reason. He drew in a deep breath. "What does that mean?" He captured her gaze and held it, this time determined to stay riveted no matter how hard his pulse pounded.

She gave a furtive glance at her friend, then back to him. "A . . . sort of a donation."

Donation? "You want to make a donation to what?"

She looked at him as if he were stupid. "I don't want to make a donation." She shook her head. "Your donation."

His donation? The conversation had gone nowhere and made no sense. "Perhaps your friend can explain it more succinctly."

Stephanie looked cornered. "This wasn't my idea. I told her she was pressing her luck."

Since the dog couldn't explain it and the animal seemed the most easy to understand, he'd have to depend on one of the humans. "Molly, what do you want me to donate?"

She drew in a deep breath as if she were going to blow out birthday candles. "Your building."

Laughter bubbled to the surface. "The building?"

She nodded. "For a dog shelter." She stepped closer, her smooth skin glowing with color. "I read an article about two women who were granted a building to use for a pet shelter for only a dollar a year. An animal shelter is a worthy cause. You could get a tax break, too."

Her words ran together in one long gush of sound.

"I told you about Teacher's Pet, and I could continue the program from this building. I could help learning-disabled kids from other schools in the evenings and summer also and protect abused and abandoned dogs at the same time."

62

Her eyes pleaded with him, while his mind rolled with fragments of her plea.

She drew closer, her finger plying at the buttons on her knit shirt. "Did you know that five million dogs are brought to shelters each year and 125,000 are euthanized because they can't find a home for them? Most of these dogs could have been trained and given love and become a wonderful pet for someone. That's what I want to do — socialize them so they can be placed somewhere."

"That's a tall order."

"It is, but I want to help. I want to do this as a career, but I'm not expecting to get rich with this endeavor." She halted long enough to gasp for breath. "If I earned more than a meager living from it and enough to pay for the dogs' upkeep, I could even pay rent."

She batted her eyelashes at him — not the flirtatious kind of batting, but as if she were overwhelmed with the information that exploded from her.

With his focus on her smudged forehead, Brent shuffled his feet. Molly knew nothing about business. No one gave away a building for a pet shelter. And a tax break? They'd put him in a padded cell if he even suggested this to anyone.

But how could he tell her? Her face glowed in the late afternoon sun, and her hair, a halo, radiated an aura around her innocent expression. Her eyes were filled with hope, and he'd watched her fade from fear to enthusiasm with each admission. His rejection would be like telling a child she could look at all the candy in the store, but no one would buy her any.

His pulse hadn't let up. In fact, he could feel the rapid thump in his temples. *Boom. Boom. Boom.* This woman would cause the death of him with her ridiculous scheme.

When he refocused, Brent became aware that he and Molly were alone. Apparently her friend and the dog had wandered off, leaving Molly and him in face-to-face combat. He rubbed his forehead, longing to relieve the pressure. All he'd done is dropped by to take a look at the building and speculate what they could do to entice a buyer. Frank had been correct. The building wouldn't work for condos. The commercial area didn't offer the ambience of boutiques and cafés, and the empty factory didn't lend itself to living space.

Molly took a step closer. "What do you think?"

Her whisper slipped through the cracks of his defenses. His shoulders fell as he gazed at her hopeful expression, and he reached out and brushed the grime from her forehead.

Guilt spread across her face.

His heart pressed against his rib cage. "This is a strange proposition, Molly. I don't want to disappoint you, but this building is valuable, and I can't consent to giving it away."

"I didn't ask you to give it to me. Only to let me use it."

He planted his feet firmly beneath them. "That's what I meant."

"If it's so valuable, then why haven't you sold it? No one's buying factories. Businesses are moving out of the area, not into it."

His stomach twisted. "We will sell it." He arched an eyebrow, facing the horrendous feeling that he'd become the villain. "And it's really not any of your concern."

She wavered backward. "It's because you don't like dogs, isn't it?"

"No." His voice shot out, louder than he'd meant to. "It has nothing to do with that. It's a business decision."

Her gaze bored into his conscience, and he was at a loss for words.

She took another backward step. "I think it does have something to do with it, and

65

whatever happened to make you hate dogs should be put to rest. Dogs don't need to forgive. Their love is unconditional. You said it yourself. We can all learn from our pets." She turned to face the gate and then looked back over her shoulder. "Thanks anyway, but I'm not giving up hope. I'll figure out something."

She marched toward the street while he stood watching her and feeling like one of those abused dogs she talked about. Faithfulness. Unconditional love. The woman lived in a dream world. He'd lived in reality and experienced things that she didn't seem to comprehend.

No matter what he told himself, the idea of dreams filled Brent's mind. A few dreams might add some excitement to his life . . . as impossible as it seemed.

Monday after school, Molly headed into the public library. Ideas had been clicking in her mind through the weekend, and she sensed the library could provide her with some ammunition to continue the battle with Brent. She tossed the word *battle* from her vocabulary. Brent had every right to defend his building, but instead of weapons, she needed facts, like a good defense attorney — raw information, data about his company, statistics about building sales in the community, plain old facts. She wanted to know everything she could and the people who could help her convince him.

Molly parked and turned off the engine. It wasn't as if she hadn't looked at other buildings. Some were too large, some too upscale, some too small. Brent's building had caught her attention for two reasons — the name Runyan, which reminded her of Randy, and then she scrutinized the size of the building and the space around it. The zoning was right. She sensed it was a perfect fit.

She'd prayed about the building and longed for God to bless her dream, but she feared He might not grant her wish. She'd turned her back on Him years ago. Maybe God chose to turn His back on her now.

Tears pushed behind her eyes, and she squeezed her eyelids closed to hold them back. Molly knew better. The Lord knew she'd repented, and she'd done all she could to atone for the hurt she'd caused her parents and herself. She needed to get a grip on her thoughts. Patience. Perseverance. That's what it took. She'd come to the library to find information, and if God wanted her dream to come true, He would be with her today. She drew in a deep breath and stepped from the car.

Inside the library, the clerk at the information desk directed her to the computer area. She slipped into a chair, logged on and opened a search engine. Her fingers flew, typing in Runyan Industrial Tool Corporation. A few references appeared — Brent's connection with the chamber of commerce and a business advertisement. That didn't help.

She leaned back, recalling that she still had the Realtor's telephone number. Calling there might tell her something. But instead of giving up, Molly became more determined. Come on. Think. Her mind flew, capturing possibilities and discarding bad ideas. Finally she took the best hunch and entered *Rochester, Michigan company profiles* into the search window, and a long list of sites filled the screen. She opened the first as a test. Her pulse skipped as she eyed the information provided: location, financial information, corporate statistics and, best of all, the board of directors.

She clicked back and moved her cursor down the list, scanning page to page until she reached the R's — Ralston Corporation, Reigers Lawn and Garden, Roger's Roost Restaurant. The cursor flew as she dragged it downward and then stopped. Runyan Industrial Tool Corporation.

She hit the hyperlink and the page opened. Her gaze landed on the address and then shifted to the corporate directors. President Morris Runyan, Director Brent Runyan, Business Manager Frank Capatelli. Perfect. The news skittered down her arms and back before she refocused on the list of names. Who was Morris Runyan? Brent's brother? His father?

She released a puff of air from between her lips. She'd assumed Brent was the company owner, but maybe she was wrong. Could it be Brent Runyan wasn't the ultimate decision maker? She dragged her teeth across her top lip and thought, but before leaving the page, Molly jotted down the address and phone number of the company offices and added Morris and Frank Capatelli to the list. With the new information, she felt hope. Her shoulders straightened. Morris Runyan might be as stiff backed as Brent, but she could try.

She entered Morris Runyan into the search window and clicked the "go" button. Numerous hyperlinks rose on the page. Morris Runyan is honored by the chamber of commerce, Morris Runyan purchases a new building, Morris Runyan's quote about small businesses in the *Detroit Free Press*,

Morris Runyan retires.

Retired? Her newfound hope sank. If he were no longer the company president, then maybe Brent had been given the position. Molly stopped herself. She was speculating. She moved the cursor to the search window and then stopped when another hyperlink caught her eye. Funeral of Randall Runyan, son of Morris Runyan, owner of . . . Molly's head lurched backward. Randall? Randy? Could this be the boy that she'd taught in elementary school? Her fingers trembled as she clicked on the link. An obituary. Randall, age thirty-seven. Husband to Patricia and father to eight-year-old Randall Junior. That had been almost four years ago.

The newspaper write-up answered her question. Randy Jr. was the student she'd had in special education. He would be Brent's nephew. Curious about Randall's death, Molly typed his name into the search window and perused the links. A newspaper article from November 2005 answered her question. A hunting accident. He'd been shot. Could that be the dark look she witnessed in Brent's eyes? Death of a brother would be difficult, but four years had passed, and why would he still be —

Stop. She shook her head, angry at herself

for trying to relate to a sibling's death. She'd never experienced a tragedy like his. She knew from her psychology classes that each person grieved in their own way. Brent had a right to take as long as he needed.

But was that the problem?

Uplifted by her research success, Molly closed the program, gathered her notes and strode outside, eager to get busy. A quick call to the Realtor could give her information on a pending sale of the Runyan building, and then, onto her most important contact. She wanted to know more about Morris Runyan, and her best source would be Rob Dyson.

Brent tried to sink lower into the overstuffed chair in his father's home office. His dad peered at him over bushy eyebrows, a look Brent had grown to recognize as dissatisfaction, and he could only assume it regarded the unsold building. Molly. She exasperated him, but her idea wasn't bad. He could just give up and offer her the use of the building. They weren't selling it anyway. Perhaps he should tell his father about the idea. Though unorthodox, his father might think the possibility creative. At least he'd get a little credit for thinking of something original. Brent's pride flared, knowing everything else at the company had been running with the precision of a well-calibrated machine.

His father shifted a stack of papers from the middle of his desk to the side, folded his hands together and leaned forward, his expression never changing. "Let's get down to business."

Brent drew in a breath. "If it's the empty building, I've been thinking of innovative ideas. I had a talk with Frank and —"

"That's another matter, Brent." His forehead knitted tighter. "This is family business."

"Family business?" Brent regretted the surprise in his voice. "Is something wrong? You're not ill, are you?"

"Do I look ill?"

Brent flinched. Morris Runyan looked as staunch as his name. "No. I just asked."

"It's Randy. He needs more than I can give him."

Randy. Air spewed from Brent's lungs. He licked his lips, searching for a response. What could he offer the boy? But then what could his father? His dad was seventy, and though he had the energy of a man many years younger, his age separated him dramatically from his eleven-year-old grandson.

His father leaned closer. "Did you hear me?"

Brent pulled his scattered thoughts together. "Randy needs more than I can give him, too."

"So we throw him out in the cold? He's your nephew."

"He's your — I know he's my nephew, Dad, but what do you suggest? Military school?"

His father's hand hit the desk with a bang. "Military school? The boy's eleven. He's withdrawing more every day, and if you spent more time with him, you'd see that. He's not the disruptive little boy he used to be when Randall died and the child's mother abandoned him. He needs attention."

Brent envisioned his long hours at work and his professional commitments. Where could he find more time for Randy than he already gave him? "I take him on weekends. I've taken him camping." Brent's shoulders sank. "I hate camping. I've tried to involve him in the Boy's Club. He doesn't socialize. I try —"

His father rose and strode across the room and back, as if pacing revved his motor. He stopped and gave Brent a dark look. "Your mother's gone, Brent. I'm alone here, missing her and struggling to be a father and mother to the boy. Your mother had mater-

73

nal instincts, but I don't know how to relate to him." His eyes pierced Brent's. "You're much closer in age than I am. I don't know what to tell you, but Randy needs to spend more time with you."

"You have a housekeeper here when you're not home. What happens when Randy's sick and has to leave school? I'm working."

"He can come here then. Don't look for trouble. I just think he can relate to you more. He needs diversions — something fun for kids. I can't play basketball. You can put up a hoop." He bounced an imaginary ball and looped it into the air.

A grin stretched Brent's taunt expression. "Not bad, Dad. You made a basket."

A faint smile flashed on his father's face before his serious look returned. He headed back toward Brent and rested his hand on the back of the chair. "Son, I know Randy's been our concern since the tragedy happened. Neither one of us is at fault, but the problem fell in our laps, and with your mom gone, I'm just asking you to give it a try. Randy needs loving care, and I don't know how to give an eleven-year-old what he needs."

Brent's stomach knotted. *Neither one of us is at fault.* If only that were true, and despite trying to convince himself otherwise, Brent believed he had jinxed his brother. God answered the prayer he'd spoken as a boy, and Brent believed his prayer had caused mayhem.

He gripped the chair arm. "I have no idea how to be a father to Randy."

"You learn. That's what all parents do. They learn."

"How, Dad? How do you learn to be a parent?"

"You make mistakes and try to do better next time. People train to be whatever they set their minds to. You can learn to be a dad to Randy."

Learn to be a dad. Brent monitored his voice. "I'll do what I can. Maybe if Randy stays with me more, maybe . . ." He faltered and glanced toward the foyer. "Where is he?"

"Where he always is. In his room. He lives there. He even eats meals there half the time. That's why I'm asking for your help. He's withdrawing more every day, and he seems so depressed."

His father's voice wavered, and Brent's worry rose. "It's going on four years. I'd hoped he would have adjusted."

"We both did, but it's not happening." His father sank into a chair.

Brent shifted and rose. "I'll go upstairs

and talk with him."

"Please do. The boy needs to know he's loved . . . even if it's by two men who aren't very good at it."

Brent nodded, accepting the truth. Molly's words wrapped around him. Everyone needed to feel loved.

Brent headed up the stairs, asking himself where God was — this loving Father who seemed to pick and choose who to bless. Jesus said let the children come to me, but not this time. Randy had gotten the short end of the stick.

Molly slipped the telephone receiver into the cradle and wiped the perspiration from her palms. She'd done it, and on Memorial Day. She'd taken a chance, using every ounce of courage she had, but her mission had been accomplished. She'd called Morris Runyan, and for some crazy reason, he had agreed to see her. He had no plans for the day, either.

Standing for a moment to grasp what she'd done, Molly reviewed their conversation. She'd said little, only that she had an interest in their unoccupied building.

"You'll have to talk with our Realtor," he'd said, his tone cautious.

"But this is a different kind of proposition, Mr. Runyan. I'd like to explain it to you in person."

"Who are you again?"

She'd wished she had some fancy title that would have impressed him, but she wouldn't lie. "My name is Molly Manning. I'm a special-education teacher at Montgomery Middle School."

Silence filled the line for a minute, and Molly's heart twisted.

"My grandson went to school in that district a few years ago. Randall Runyan."

"I remember him. He was a puzzle. You know what I mean?" Molly wanted to kick herself for being so blunt.

"How do you mean?"

She swallowed, grasping a second to form the right words. "He was in special education, but I never felt he belonged there. He had discipline problems, but he seemed bright to me."

Morris Runyan made a sound almost like an exasperated chuckle. "I agree, Miss Manning. He needed something that special education couldn't offer."

She started to ask what he meant, then stopped. No more careless comments or questions.

"Would you like to come by this evening?" he'd asked.

She muffled her cheer of joy. "I'll be there," she'd said. And now she stood in her kitchen, wondering how to dress. Should she dress like a professional or go as she was — a woman who loved dogs and kids and had a dream that Morris Runyan could help her reach.

Molly settled for a pair of beige slacks and a coral-colored knit top. She slung her shoulder bag over her arm and headed to the door, reeling with anticipation.

On the highway, she rehearsed what she would say, changing it every half mile when she thought of something more impressive or something that she suspected Mr. Runyan would find more important. She wanted to stress the tax write-off, but then she thought maybe she should first approach his charitable nature. Finally she sent up a prayer and decided to put it in God's hands because hers often made a mess of things. How could someone who prided herself on quality end up making so many mistakes? Brent's face dropped into her thoughts. She'd certainly failed there.

When she pulled in front of his house on Lake Angelus, she paused a moment, eyeing the impressive home and garnering her courage. *Be yourself, Molly. Speak from your heart.* She wasn't sure where the advice came from, but she knew what she'd heard had wisdom. She turned the steering wheel and rolled up the driveway, her heart in her throat.

The Greek Revival entrance intimidated her. She felt out of place with its formal appearance, white Doric columns and sloping cornice above the loggia. Could the man inside be as cold and reserved? Her gaze swept over the surroundings again, particularly the appealing landscaping that added a bit of color to the grounds. She could only hope Morris Runyan had the same charm.

Molly strode up the two steps to the front door and pushed the bell. She anticipated a butler or housekeeper opening the door, but her expectation ended when she looked into the same midnight-blue eyes of Brent Runyan, camouflaged by bushy eyebrows.

"Miss Manning?"

His strong voice surprised her. "Yes. Mr. Runyan?"

He nodded.

"Thank you for seeing me tonight. I hadn't expected you to be so kind."

"Why not?" he said, pushing back the door for her to enter.

His brusque response echoed Brent's terse responses. Genetic, she feared. She didn't know how to respond, so she tossed out the first thing that entered her mind. "It's a holiday."

The foyer extended to the back of the house, where she caught the glimpse of a fireplace, and to her left, the living room spread beyond the broad archway, flanked by a staircase to the second floor. Morris motioned her into the living room, and when she entered, the elegant decor centered on another massive fireplace.

"Please have a seat." He motioned toward an easy chair beside the hearth.

Molly sank into the chair as tension caught up with her. She folded her hands in her lap to control the tremble that had appeared without warning. "Your home is lovely, Mr. Runyan."

"Thank you," he said, his eyes searching her face.

Her mouth had dried to sawdust.

Morris folded his hands in his lap. "So, talk to me, Miss Manning."

"Please call me Molly." She unknotted her fingers and spread them apart, aching to relax. "It's a long story, but first I'll give you some basic information." She drew in a breath and told him how she'd begun the Teacher's Pet program and her dream of being a veterinarian.

"So what stopped you? Finances?"

The question caught her off guard, and for a moment horrible memories flooded her mind. Her lying and cheating. The drinking, the — She pushed her head above the torrent. She'd told the acceptable short version of her story often. "My biggest problem was the college tests. Universities that offer veterinary medicine education are limited in the U.S. and so they only take the top students — 4.0 GPA with the highest college-entry test scores. I did well in school, but I couldn't compete with my test scores."

A deep frown settled on his face. "I see." He shifted his hands and tapped his index finger on the chair arm, making a soft rhythmic thud. "Veterinary assistant? That wouldn't be quite so demanding."

She lowered her head, thinking of her promise to God to be the best she could be. "I don't settle for second-rate. I still have dreams. They've changed, but I want to run a dog shelter. I don't suppose you're aware of the large number of abandoned and abused dogs struggling to survive, but they can be trained to be excellent —"

"Saving dogs is important to you?" She looked at him and nodded. "Now tell me. How does the building on Rochester Road come into this?"

"I need a building for the shelter, and one preferably zoned for commerce and not residential. Your building is perfect, and it's large enough to run the Teacher's Pet program."

"So you want to rent this building?"

Her heart slipped to her toes, and her shoulders weighted with her next sentence. "I can't afford to rent a building. Not now."

He drew back, his eyes narrowing again. "You want us to give you the building? We can't consider —"

"No, not give, just let us use it for . . . a small sum to make it legal. Maybe, ten dollars? I read an article —"

"As much as ten dollars." Morris's eyes widened. This time he tapped his index finger against his chin. "Hmm?"

His playful expression made her chuckle, and to her pleasure, he joined her. With his changed demeanor, her fears eased.

Morris's grin faded. "Why do you think it wouldn't be more lucrative for me to sell the building?"

"Because it hasn't sold in over two years. I talked to the Realtor. By giving me use of the building, you'd receive a charitable donation tax write-off, and you'd be doing something to help resolve a serious problem for abandoned animals."

His head jolted backward. "You talked with the Realtor?"

"Yes." She waited, hoping he wouldn't be angry.

"Very enterprising of you." He surveyed her a moment before he muttered, "That must have been what Brent was talking about."

Her pulse zinged when she heard his name. Talking about what? Her or the building? "You might not like dogs."

"Why would you think that?"

Her arms turned to ice thinking of Brent's attitude. Finally she shrugged. "I just assumed —"

"I had two sons, Miss . . . Molly. My youngest begged for a dog, and I allowed him to have one with stipulations." His eyes darkened.

Stipulations? What did that mean?

"You know kids. He followed the rules at first but then . . ."

His voice faded and she waited until the silence became unbearable. "What happened?"

"I had to —" His face blanched, and he looked down. "Toby ran away."

"Toby was the dog?"

"A golden retriever. A hunting dog."

Air shot from Molly's lungs. "I'm sorry. I

know it's hard to lose pets. Your youngest was —"

"Brent. He didn't handle it well."

And obviously still doesn't. "Loss is difficult for children." That couldn't be all the story. Adults adjust.

He rose and brushed his fingers over his chin. "Down to business." He dug out a cell phone from his pocket and sank back into his chair. "Let me make a quick call."

Molly's pulse thumped in her temple. She tried to take a deep calming breath while her attention had riveted to the phone.

Morris hit the numbers and waited. When someone answered, he gave a nod. "Brent. Yesterday you brought up the building on Rochester Road, but we never got back to it. Any progress on selling the thing?"

Knots tied Molly's muscles in bunches.

Morris listened a moment while Molly searched at his face. "If that's the case, let's try a new tack." He paused.

Molly strained to hear Brent's side of the conversation. She heard his voice but couldn't make out the words.

"Wait a minute." Morris's hand shot upward. "Let me tell you my idea." He gave Molly a wink. "Let's use the building for a worthy cause."

"Worthy cause?" Brent's voice sailed from

the receiver like a megaphone. "Don't tell me . . ."

Molly heard the disbelief in his voice. She closed her eyes and cringed. She'd envisioned this differently.

"Don't tell you what?" But Morris didn't wait for his answer. "Why not check with the Realtor? Our agreement with them should have expired by now anyway."

Her pulse accelerated. Molly closed her eyes and clamped her hands to the cushion of her chair.

"I have a young lady here, and I'd like to have you talk with her."

"I knew it," burst from the telephone. "Why couldn't she have waited?"

Wait for what? Molly wondered.

"Who are you talking about, Brent? I think you'll like this young woman's ideas. Remember how much you loved Toby. She wants space for a dog shelter."

"Don't tell me, Dad." Morris held the telephone from his ear, a scowl embedding his face. "Is the lovely young woman named Molly Manning?" Morris's eyes shifted to Molly.

She flinched.

"Yes, it is. How did you know?" He listened again, his look intense. "And you didn't like the idea?"

85

Feeling like a snake, Molly squirmed in the chair.

Exasperation filled Morris's face. "Oh, then you like the idea?" He listened for a moment than shook his head. "Well, apparently you didn't like it when you talked with her."

Molly looked toward the doorway, wishing she could escape, but she sensed she was on the doorstep of change. Either her dream was about to come true or it had blown up in her face. She couldn't tell from Morris's expression.

When Brent's father disconnected and turned to face her, Molly knew she had some explaining to do.

CHAPTER FOUR

Brent jammed the telephone receiver onto the cradle and sat back in his chair. Why hadn't Molly waited? His stomach knotted. He'd planned to present the idea to his father on Tuesday. Instead Randy ended up being the topic of the evening, and he'd let the business topic slip. He expected Molly's determination, but he hadn't expected shrewdness.

He rose from the desk and strode across the great room. Night had settled across the sky, and he stood staring into the darkness, his mind flying from problem to problem. He'd made progress with his father recently. His father had stepped back and allowed him to run the business. Finally. Tonight's setback destroyed that. Now his proposal for the building had become his father's baby instead of his. He'd worked hard to set himself up as the spokesman and decision maker for the company, and today

Molly had undone his efforts. He wrestled between admiring Molly's determination and being irritated.

Tonight irritation won out. The woman could wrangle a cobra with her innocent look.

A loud thud stopped Brent cold. He glanced up toward the ceiling and then hurried to the staircase. "Randy. What's going on?"

No response.

"Are you okay?"

Another *bam.*

He darted up the stairs two at a time and swung past the laundry room to the front bedroom doorway. He grasped the knob and then stopped himself. "Randy, are you okay?"

"Yes."

Brent counted to ten and added another five for good measure. "May I come in?"

"No."

"Randy, please."

Behind the door a softer thud resounded. "What?"

"I'd like to come in." He waited, not wanting to destroy the little trust he'd developed with Randy. This room was the boy's, and he'd agreed it was to be off-limits except for an emergency. Now for the definition of *emergency.* He had rules and —

The door swung open, and he looked into a face distorted with frustration and red around his eyes as if Randy had been crying.

He looked past the boy into his bedroom. The typical unmade bed and clothes scattered on the floor didn't bother him. What did concern him was Randy's desk chair, which lay toppled on the floor along with a book. The laptop he'd given him to use for his schoolwork was open, but the screen saver made it impossible for Brent to see what he'd been reading. "What's wrong?"

The boy shrugged.

"Can I come in?"

Randy stepped back and then walked toward the toppled chair and set it upright.

Brent followed behind and sat on the edge of his rumpled bed, noticing Randy's school books on the floor. "Trouble with your homework?"

"No." He jerked his arm and bumped the keyboard.

The screen saver vanished, and Brent could see the monitor. E-mail. But the words were too distant to read.

Randy noticed him looking and realized what he'd done. He shifted his body to cover the screen.

Though the purpose of the laptop was to provide Randy help with homework, Brent had allowed him limited e-mail access when he'd been befriended by one boy from his school. Brent wanted to encourage the friendship. Maybe e-mail privileges had been a mistake. "Did an e-mail upset you?"

"No." He fidgeted in the chair.

Something in an e-mail had caused this problem, despite what Randy had said.

Brent swiped a piece of lint from his eyelash and motioned toward the computer. "Who's that from?"

Randy shifted even farther.

"Something's wrong, Randy. Have you had a fight with your friend?"

He shook his head. "It's not from my friend."

Brent rose from the bed. "Then who is it?"

Randy shrugged.

"Did he say something to upset you?"

Randy spun on his chair, making an attempt to delete the message, but Brent got there before he did and covered the board with his hand. He leaned over the boy and read the message. He released a breath and shook his head. "How did this person get your e-mail address?"

"I don't know."

"Do you know who this is?" He looked at the e-mail address. "You don't know this e-mail address? Who's this 'koolkid' guy?"

"I don't know."

Brent peered at the e-mail's vicious comments — *stupid, mental* and some filthy words Brent didn't want to think about.

He rose, wanting so badly to take Randy in his arms, but he couldn't. Hugging the boy seemed inappropriate, and a handshake didn't fit the situation either. "Words can't hurt us, Randy, especially words that aren't true."

"I am stupid."

"You're none of those things." Brent felt helpless. He looked at the boy's downtrodden expression.

"Some kids call me Special Ed. I don't want to be in those classes."

The boy needed to know he was special in other ways, not special because he was dumb, but Brent didn't know how to express it. "I don't think you're any of those things."

Randy kicked his heel against the chair leg. "I don't need anybody."

Brent longed for words that could make a difference, but he had none. His father's words came back to him. *Learn to be a dad.* He could run a business better than his dad gave him credit, but he didn't know how to be a father to Randy.

He rested his hand on his nephew's shoulder. "I need you, Randy."

The boy lifted his face to Brent, his eyes exploring his as if seeking the truth, and a surprising quiet fell over him. Where those words came from, Brent didn't question. They'd worked.

Randy stared at the wooden floor, his toe tracing the lines of a board joint over and over. When he looked up, moisture clung to the corners of his eyes. "Why?"

Why? Brent released a ragged breath, searching for a reason. "Because I get lonely without a friend. It's nice to have someone here to talk with and share a meal."

"I eat up here."

"But I hope you'll come down one day." His hand shifted from the chair back and rested on Randy's shoulder.

The boy twitched at his touch, but then relaxed.

He gave Randy's shoulder a squeeze. "What do you say? School will be over in a couple of weeks, and we'll find some fun things to do. Would you like me to put up a basketball hoop?"

Randy gave a one-shoulder shrug. "I'm probably too short."

"I can fix that, and I'm not very good, either. I'm sure you'll beat me."

"Beat you? Why?" His face grew curious.

"Because your dad was good at basketball. He played on the team in high school."

His eyes brightened. "He did?"

"He did." Brent swallowed forcing out the next sentence. "I could tell you lots of things about your dad."

Randy straightened in the chair. "Like what?"

"He liked to hunt. Did you know that?" Brent's heart ached as the words fell from his mouth.

"Hunt what?"

"Let's go down and have some ice cream, and I'll tell you."

"Okay."

Brent's feet felt weighted as he headed for the door. The boy knew so little about his dad, and no one had told him anything. What had they been thinking?

Randy followed behind Brent as he took the stairs to the first floor. Molly popped into his mind as always. He wondered how she would handle Randy. Did she have the innate ability to be a mother, like women seemed to have? He guessed she could. Molly could do just about anything. He had to stop thinking about her. Tonight Randy required his attention. The boy needed him even more than Molly needed his building.

"Will you go with me?" Molly leaned against the door frame and studied Steph. "Please. I need your support."

Steph placed her hands on her hips. "Did you tell him I was coming when you called him?" She closed one eye and peered at her. "Be honest."

"I'm always honest. In fact, that gets me into trouble."

"You're right." Steph waited. "Answer my question."

"No, but —"

"But nothing. I'm not going to show up and —"

"Then will you just ride with me?" When Steph got stubborn, which she didn't do often, Molly knew she was in trouble. "You can wait in the office while I go in." She pressed her palms together as if she were praying. "Please."

Steph shook her head. "You look pathetic."

"I am. I need you."

"Right." She motioned Molly toward the doorway. "Let's get this over with."

Molly gave her a hug and bolted out the door. Brent said he'd be at the office until

6:00 p.m., and her watch warned her that she needed to hurry. Edging on the speed limit, Molly pulled into the Runyan parking lot at three minutes to six.

"Hurry," she said, feeling out of breath. She hit the lock button as Steph slammed the passenger door. When Molly reached the outer office, the room was empty and Brent's office door was closed. She bolted across the floor and knocked.

No sound came through the barrier.

"Mr. Runyan." She rapped louder as her heart sank. She turned to Steph. "He's gone."

Steph looked at the wall clock and checked her watch. "It's ten minutes after six, according to their clock." She motioned toward the wall.

Molly turned toward the outside door, her legs so heavy she sensed they'd been bound with twenty-pound weights. "I thought he'd wait."

"You thought wrong." Steph slipped her arm around Molly's shoulders. "He doesn't care about your dream, Molly."

"I know." She looked at the empty secretary desk, then at the open door. "Let's go." As she took a step, the obvious struck her as her spirit soared. "If he's gone, then why isn't the outer door locked?"

Steph halted beside her. "Good point."

Adrenaline rushed to action. "Maybe he's —"

Motion caught her from the corridor doorway, and Molly froze.

"Molly." He stood in the doorway, holding a stack of papers.

"We had an appointment."

Brent lowered his eyes. "Not really. You asked if you could see me in the late afternoon."

Apparently he didn't interpret her request as an appointment. "I thought I had an appointment." She glanced at his closed door and remembered the time. "Can we talk now?"

She heard his ragged exhale as he lifted his gaze to hers. His expression was unreadable, a mixture of disappointment, exasperation and hurt. Her pulse skipped when she saw the emotion that filled his eyes.

"Molly, I'm trying to be patient. I understand how much a dog shelter means to you and how determined you are, but you don't realize what you've done."

She squirmed beneath his gaze.

Brent took a step forward then stopped. "My father isn't the only say in business matters. You should have waited."

Molly's chest felt heavy. "I'm sorry. I was

desperate."

His jaw tightened. "No more desperate than I am."

His comment threw her off. She studied his face, wishing she knew what he was thinking. "Your father said you had a dog you loved. Toby."

Brent was startled. "My father should — that has nothing to do with the property."

"But it does." She stepped closer. "I can't force you to love my project, but if you've had any feelings for dogs, please give my idea some thought. You could drop by Teacher's Pet any Wednesday about 1:00 p.m. and observe the class. You'd see how we teach the animals obedience. Dogs are very smart, and they have attributes that many people want but don't have."

He gave his head a shake as if he thought she was an idiot. "I've seen dogs chase cats up trees, but I never wanted that attribute."

Beneath his ire, Molly sensed a new emotion. Her pulse kicked. "The world would be a better place if we were all partly dogs."

"Molly, I have things to do tonight. I need to leave. I can't deal with this problem. If you want —"

She drew back, feeling as if he'd opened a side gate and let her pet dog loose in traffic.

Steph touched her arm. "Molly, let's go."

Her eyes were pleading.

Molly gave a final look at Brent. "Sorry I bothered you."

Brent lifted his hand. "Molly, please . . ."

She motioned for Steph to go ahead, and she followed with her tail between her legs.

Molly looked forward to Wednesday, but today she didn't look forward to anything. The weekend had been a bust. All she could think of was her useless talk with Brent on Monday, and since then the past two days had dragged with each infinitesimal emotion. She reviewed her tack and realized she'd made a grave error. From Brent's expression, she sensed tension between him and his father.

What she'd done is alienated herself from Brent by dragging his father into the situation. Why hadn't she waited? He'd said the same to her. She shouldn't have pushed like she always did, never considering the damage she could do but always so certain she was right.

She'd prayed for patience, but she supposed God expected her to make an effort as well. Molly knew her flaws all too well. She had many, but she'd focused on doing good and making her life worthy of God's blessings. A prayer flew heavenward that

God would look at her heart and guide her.

The school day had dragged. She barely tasted what she ate of her lunch, and now her enthusiasm for the class she loved had dampened. How long could she keep Teacher's Pet going in a school setting? Would the shelter administrator continue to loan her the dogs and go through the hassle of bringing them to the school each week? Without them, her program would fail. She sent up another prayer, thanking God for the shelter's support.

Drawing up her shoulders, she grabbed her classroom notes and headed down the corridor. She had eight students who needed her to be spirited and teach them life skills. Her own problems needed to be leashed and tied to a tree. As she entered, their voices overwhelmed her. Working with special needs students meant capturing their interest and then keeping it, which was no easy trick.

"In your seats," Molly said, her index fingers touching her lips. "Other students in this building need to hear their teachers, and we have work to do."

Chairs scraped along the floor, someone swished a book onto the floor followed by a poke, and two boys nose-dived to retrieve the books.

"You don't want me to send the dogs back to the shelter, do you?"

Eight faces turned to her. "Why?" one student asked.

"If we don't have time to cover our class work, then that's the option. Remember, I give you choices. That's a little different than how we train the dogs."

One eager student, Meg, waved her hand. "Yes, because we can make smart decisions."

Molly nodded. "Everyone can make wise choices."

"Dogs can think." Adam's voice cut through the air. "They're smarter than some people."

Brent popped into Molly's mind and she agreed. "Dogs are very smart, but they can get confused with choices sometimes just like we do." She looked at each of them as she realized that she'd confused Brent. What's more, she'd bombarded him without regard to protocol.

Noise grew in the room, and Molly got a grip on herself. "Today we're going to talk about things we can learn from a dog." Somehow she led the discussion on attributes, hoping they could see that they had also learned some of these qualities. She watched the time tick by. Finally the class ended and they left the room and headed for the large multipurpose room.

Once there, Adam headed for the exit door and opened it. Outside, Molly saw the shelter's van. "Does everyone have a leash?"

The students waved the leashes while a couple cracked them like whips.

"Careful." She motioned them toward her. "Line up and we'll bring in the dogs one by one."

Struggling to stay focused, Molly asked an adult volunteer to keep the line moving and headed to the center of the room. As she reviewed her teaching notes, an office secretary stepped through the corridor door and beckoned her.

"You have a visitor." She pointed behind her. "Is it okay if he comes in?"

He? Molly's heart stood still. She shifted closer to the doorway and saw Brent standing in the hallway. "It's fine." Her voice sounded breathless.

The secretary motioned him inside and left, closing the door.

Molly watched as Brent strode toward her. He looked uneasy. Seeing him that way, she pulled herself together and filled her lungs. "Thank you for coming. I can't tell you how much this means to me."

He scanned the room and then focused

on the students.

"This part of the class is hands-on. School ends in two weeks, so this is their last chance to prepare for graduation. The shelter staff who houses the dogs will test their skills. Then if all looks good, they'll be adopted or at least will go to a foster home until they can be adopted."

His gaze finally settled on her. "Molly, I'm sorry about Monday. I know I hurt you and —"

She ached, seeing his discomfort. "I'm sorry, too." She glanced over her shoulder at the students. "I need to get started." She pointed to a stack of chairs piled against one wall. "Have a seat anywhere."

He studied her as if he had more to say, but instead he ambled toward the chairs.

Molly turned her attention to the children, hoping to make a good impression on Brent. If he understood what her program could do, he'd want to support it. If she had her own shelter, she could train more dogs so that they were socialized to be adopted or live with foster families, and she could invite the best students from her groups to work part-time. Another win-win situation. The animals would receive good training and the kids would feel purposeful and earn money at the same time. The experience would give them confidence and self-esteem."

Her gaze drifted back to Brent, who watched her from across the room. Her heart lurched.

Lord, help the kids shine today. This is not as much for me, but for the kids and the dogs. They need to be loved.

So did she.

Brent sat on the hard chair, his discomfort rising each second. He'd been rash to stop and give her hope. His motive was selfish. Randy needed something to draw him out of himself, and if Molly was right, something like this might work.

Randy was about the age of these kids, but Randy's school didn't have a program like this. A school psychologist had diagnosed Randy with ADHD. But Brent suspected no one had really put a finger on Randy's condition. One thing he'd noticed since he'd tried to be more like a dad is that when he gave Randy his undivided attention, the boy's behavior improved.

A black Lab pulled away from a student, his leash dragging across the floor while the girl chased after him. The dog headed straight for Brent. Before he could stand, the dog plopped a paw on each knee and swiped his tongue across Brent's turned cheek.

"Get down," Brent said, trying to grab the leash.

The girl grasped the strap from him. "Teddy. Off."

The dog stepped down and sat in front of him.

"Good boy, Teddy." The girl ruffled his head and handed him a small piece of dry dog food.

"Good boy," Brent repeated and then looked up at the girl. "You did a nice job."

"You didn't."

His head jerked back. He reminded himself she was a special needs student.

" 'Get down' confuses a dog. 'Down' means lay on the floor. They don't even know what 'get' means." She stared him straight in the eyes. "You have to say 'off.' Trained dogs know that."

Brent wanted to laugh. "Thank you. I'll remember that."

"Good." She stood there a moment and then extended the leash. "Want to walk him?"

"Meg."

Molly's firm voice surprised Brent.

She looked at the girl with a scowl as she strutted across the floor. "You need to join

104

the class. Next week we have more visitors who'll watch how well you work with the dogs. You need to practice."

"I know," the girl said as she drew the leash tighter and headed back to the center of the room with Teddy at her heels.

Molly dug her hands into her pockets. "Sorry. They're supposed to keep a tight rein on them."

"It's okay, Molly. She really did a nice job. She even gave me a little lesson."

"I hope she wasn't rude."

Rude? He thought about the way he'd treated Molly. The student had been no ruder than he'd been. "Blunt, not rude."

She bit the corner of her lip and backed away, tilting her head toward the students. "I need to get back to work."

So did he, but he didn't move. He watched Molly with the kids — loving but firm, teaching and rewarding. Brent lowered his head, thinking of his father's orders to learn to be a dad. He had much to learn about discipline and everything to learn about loving.

CHAPTER FIVE

Brent wants to talk with me.

Molly peered at the text message and reread it. *Call me about Teacher's Pet.* She pressed her cell phone against her chest, her heart hammering against her palm.

Dreams were for dreaming, but some were for living. Molly's hope rose. Maybe her heart's desire could become a reality. She closed her eyes to stem her tears and then opened them again to eye the wall clock. She counted the minutes before lunch. Her students' questions swirled in her mind until she could sort them and answer as she always did. The note barraged her thoughts, and she couldn't let it go.

The bell sounded. Students gathered their materials and put books away, then scampered out the door. Some lagged behind with last-minute questions or feared leaving the sanctity of the classroom, where they knew they were accepted. No matter what problem hampered them, some students enjoyed raising their own self-esteem by putting down others. She tried to teach them to respect everyone, but sometimes she failed.

"See you tomorrow, Roxie." She waved at one of her newest students, a transfer from out of state.

Molly closed the door and stepped away from the bustle of the corridor where lockers clanged and students called out insults as they passed each other. No wonder her job seemed endless.

Near the window, she pulled her cell phone from her pants pocket and hit the number and waited.

It rang twice and then stopped. She eyed her cell phone display. *Call failed.* She sank into the chair, clutching the phone, and tried again.

Call failed.

Slamming her hand on her desk, Molly pressed her forehead against the wood. She could picture Brent's deep blue eyes, the occasional sparkle and vulnerable looks that appeared and then faded away. How deep was his wound? Could it be all over the loss of a dog or could it be something more? Something deeper?

A sigh fluttered from her lungs, and she

lifted her head. The clock warned her that lunchtime was passing. She couldn't eat anyway, so what was the difference? She stood and slipped the telephone into her pocket and sank back into her chair.

Brent heard the familiar jingle of his cell phone and dug it from his pocket. He read the caller ID. Molly, and on his cell phone. That confused him. The men eyed him as he flipped his cell open again.

Dial tone. He read the screen. *Missed call.*

Surprised at the tug of his heart, he slipped his phone back into his pocket. In a moment, it rang again. He pulled out the phone and opened the lid. The call failed again.

He clutched the cell and rose. "Sorry. This is important." He scanned the room and headed toward a window. Hopefully he'd get a better reception. He hit Dial and Molly's numbers beeped in. After a short ring, he heard her hello.

"Molly, this is Brent Runyan. I'm sorry about missing your calls. I had to move to a window." The clang of silverware and china along with the rumble of voices nearly blocked her voice.

"I had to wait for a break to return your call. Sorry. I knew it was important."

Important. He'd never thought. Once again, his motive would disappoint her. He struggled to find his voice. "It's hard to hear, Molly. I want to ask you some questions about your program, but this isn't a good time." He felt his chest tighten. "How about dinner?"

"Dinner?"

He pushed the receiver tighter against his ear. Her single word echoed silence. Dinner may have been too much for her. "Or any time. Any place, really. You choose. I'll pick you up." He'd been too brash. She'd been anxious the last time they'd talked and so hopeful. He knew he would only disappoint her again. His mouth opened to explain.

"Okay, but," she said, ending his thought to be forthright, "meet me at Cregar's. It's a coffee shop at Crooks and Auburn Road. You'll see it."

What was this with Cregar's? Ideas clicked through his head. "Okay, but why there?"

"I want to show you something."

He heard a new lilt to her voice, and he could picture her large hazel eyes flashing the amazing sparks of green. The image squeezed against his chest. "Okay." It wasn't okay. He wanted to know what this was about.

109

Molly's voice had brightened. "I'll see you later."

"Later," he said, and the line went dead.

What happened? He'd wanted some questions answered, and suddenly she'd tangled him in one of her spur-of-the-moment adventures. Images flashed in his mind — Molly and Fred at the Rochester factory with her friend who looked as dazed as he felt; Molly teaching her class with a firm but loving hand; Molly backing away in his office when he offended her. His heart melted. She did that to him. Today she'd sidetracked him, and now he could only speculate what she had in mind for him.

He'd nearly fallen over his feet many times since he'd met her. She had a way about her. A delight he'd never seen in an adult before. Maybe he was in the wrong business. Molly loved her mission. He had no doubt about it. She'd do anything to make her dream come true, and he had to admire her for that, except he was part of that dream, and he could fail her. Business was business, and her scheme might make little sense to the board unless he could convince them otherwise.

He filled his lungs and calmed himself. When he headed for the table, his coworkers were watching. He had to finish his lunch or cause suspicion, but right now his stomach objected. His delicious steak sandwich had been swept away by a pair of hazel-green eyes.

Molly stared out the coffee shop window. Would this end with another fiasco, or would she make a point? She'd decided to take a chance again. The last one had blown up in her face, and this one could, too. She folded her hands and closed her eyes, sending up a prayer for guidance. She had no idea what Brent wanted, but she'd hoped he wanted to tell her he had worked it out and the building could be hers. Why else would he call?

But good news didn't always come her way. So while her reasoning seemed logical, in her heart she feared a failure. Molly sipped her latte, wishing she'd skipped dinner. Anxiety knotted her stomach.

A sports car pulled in, and her eyes followed it, waiting to see him step out. Her breath hitched when she saw him. Brent strode toward the door, looking purposeful. Instead of a suit, he wore a knit polo shirt that emphasized his broad chest like an endless sea of deep teal blue.

She turned away from the window and focused on her drink. It was now or never.

The words sprang to her mind.

"Molly."

She looked over her shoulder and managed a smile. "Hi. Thanks for coming, Mr. Runyan." She had to catch herself every time she said his name.

"Mr. Runyan?"

He stood over her with an expression she couldn't read while the knot around her dinner squeezed it up to her throat.

"If I call you Molly, how about calling me Brent." His mouth curved to a grin. "*Mr. Runyan* belongs to my father."

Brent. The familiar name felt right. But to say it aloud to him? She managed a nod and rested her hand on her shoulder bag. "Do you want to talk now or later?"

His eyes shifted to her hand. "Let's talk later. Apparently you want to show me something." A faint scowl stole to his face. "I don't like surprises."

"It'll only take a few minutes." She felt as if she should duck. She stood and slipped her bag over her shoulder. "I'll drive. I know where we're going. It's just up the road."

He flinched, yet stepped back, allowing her to go first. She led him to her car and even opened the door for him. She smiled, but he didn't. Once on the road, they fell silent. Molly wanted to explain where they were going, but she decided to let her purpose speak for itself.

Seeing the Adams Road traffic light ahead, she looked for the building and then pulled into the parking lot and slipped the car into a space. "This is it." She jumped out and shut her door.

He didn't move.

Wondering what he was thinking but not really wanting to know, she headed around the car and opened his door. "This is it."

He pointed to the sign on the building. "Michigan Humane Society?"

"You said you wanted to talk about Teacher's Pet." She tilted her head toward the entrance. "These people cooperate with me to make the program work. We're like a team, hoping to make this a 'no-kill community.'"

He glanced away and then stepped out. "You're tenacious, Molly. You just don't give up, do you?" He grinned.

She smiled back and shook her head. "Not when it's something this important."

"Let's go. I can't wait to see what you have in store."

Molly waved at the person behind the desk as she entered, knowing she'd become a familiar face at the facility.

"We'd like to look at the dogs," she said,

flashing a secretive wink at the young man.

"Go right ahead. You know the way."

Molly beckoned Brent to follow, and though he shook his head at her, he did as she asked. He needed to see for himself the many dogs needing homes, dogs that could make wonderful pets and who would have quality lives if someone adopted them.

After closing the first door, yelps and woofs caterwauled from the room ahead of them. Sensing Brent holding back, Molly looked over her shoulder. His handsome face appeared tense, and she realized this would be another of her do-or-die escapades. If he didn't come around, she'd lose every chance of winning him over.

"I know you believe I'm underhanded, but I want you to see why I'm so determined to open a shelter. Mine would be one leaf on a tree, but it would be the tree of life for these animals. Do you realize how many dogs are lost because there's no home for them?"

"You've told me, Molly, and I —"

"I want to create a sanctuary for these animals so they can become someone's pet. I can help train them and socialize them so they can live in a loving home, and in the process, I can help children who have needs, too."

She felt tears filling her eyes, and Brent's

expression only caused them to grow. He looked wounded.

Brent touched her arm. "I wanted to talk about that, but you brought me here."

"I know, but I —" She gazed at his palm against her arm. "We're here. Let's just take a look."

Molly backed away as Brent's fingers slid from her arm. Without encouraging him to follow, she pulled herself together and marched toward the dog cages. Once inside, they were greeted with barks and tails wagging — labs, hounds, terriers, shepherds, setters — even a cute dachshund stuck its nose against the cage walls. Molly bent and petted the animal.

Brent stood in the middle of the aisle, avoiding the eager dogs on each side. Yet something caused him to turn, and he knelt beside a golden Lab and petted the dog's nose through the cage, as if in a trance.

Befuddled by his behavior, she stood beside him and waited. When he remained there, she stooped to join him. "His name is Rocket," she said, pointing to the name written on a card on the cage.

When Brent rose, his expression seemed haunted, and Molly's conscience pinged with regret. She touched his arm. "Let's go."

He eased upward, his gaze riveted to the

dog. In slow motion, he turned toward the door and followed her into the corridor.

"Let's go back to the coffee shop," she said, wanting to end the excruciating situation. What had she done?

Brent turned his back on the pitiful sight and followed Molly out of the building. If any woman could get under his skin, Molly would win the prize. She either made him want to yell or kiss her. He'd tried to keep her out of his mind, but she clung there like arsenic and honey to a spoon. Sweet, yet poison.

The golden retriever looked like Toby. It took him back to his youth, a time when he felt so unloved except by the gentle dog. Since the day Toby vanished, he hardened his heart to attachments. What else could a boy do? He'd lost his best friend. His ally.

When he thought about his youth, Randy filled his mind. Their traits were similar — the boy could have been his son. While Randy felt abandoned by his father who died and his mother who ran out on him, as a boy Brent had felt ignored and useless. Randy covered his feelings with aloofness and bad behavior, but Brent had hidden his feelings of rejection and found joy and love in his dog. His brother, Randall, had his father's strengths. He hunted and took control, fearless as a bee with its stinger ready. Brent, with his head in books and dreams, was a fly, just an irritating nuisance.

The driver's door slammed closed, and Molly waited.

Brent realized he'd been standing at the passenger side with his mind everywhere but in the present. He opened the door and slid in, wanting to apologize, but too tangled in confusion to find the words.

Molly turned the key in the ignition but didn't shift into Reverse.

He waited until the silence became unbearable and then turned toward her, wanting to break the barricade.

"Rocket reminded you of Toby," she said before he could say anything.

Her comment smacked him in the stomach, and the knot uncurled into a streamer of memories. "Yes. Very much."

"I'm sorry, Mr. . . . Brent." She faltered. "I've called you Brent in my mind all the time."

Her admission skittered through his chest. How often had she thought of him? As much as he'd thought of her? She'd become sparkles in his mind that sometimes made him grimace and sometimes caused him to smile.

"I like the sound of Brent." He'd let the truth slip. How long could he keep the chains wrapped around his heart? "It sounds right."

"It does to me, too." She shifted into Reverse, maneuvered to the road and headed back the way they'd come.

But his pleasant thoughts soon clanked into dungeonlike questions. Was Molly only manipulating him to get her hands on the property? Her determination scared him. He fought back his pessimism, and the dark question sank beneath logic. When he looked into her eyes, he witnessed only sincerity.

As the café appeared, Brent released his pent-up breath. He'd invited her tonight so they could talk, but now she'd muddied the waters with the trip to the Humane Society, and he knew she didn't suspect what he wanted. They each had a motive and each with a purpose important to them, but opposite.

"Do you still want to talk?" Molly's voice cut into his thoughts.

He looked into her eyes. "Yes, but if —"

She pulled on the door handle and was outside the car before he could finish his sentence.

They placed their order and found a small

table. Her latte smelled of cinnamon, and he took a sip of his black coffee, needing the caffeine to steady his jangled nerves.

Molly set her cup on the table and folded her hands. "You know why I came out this way. Now it's time I learn what you wanted to say."

His well-rehearsed commentary and organized questions slid into a whirlpool of discomposure. Where to begin? "Molly, I don't think this is what you wanted to hear."

Hope skittered from her face.

"I'm really here about my nephew, Randy." He squirmed in his chair, wishing he were telling her the board agreed to rent her the property for some small amount.

"You've never mentioned him, and I asked."

The hurt look on her face made him yearn to reach out and hold her in his arms. "Your question got lost in our conversation, and I didn't guide it back. Randy's a difficult topic for me, but one I need to deal with."

"Deal with?"

The edgy tone in her voice let him know what she thought. "I mean . . . Molly, it's a long story."

"I know some of it, I think. Just tell me."

He drew back, filling his lungs with air while feeling it leak out again before he could speak. He began with Randall's death, the boy's mother leaving Randy behind and Randy's life with his grandparents and then his grandfather alone. "My dad has asked me to take over, and I'm at a loss. Randy needs too much. I don't know if he's ADHD or if he's just stubborn or if —"

"Or if he's scared or lonely or hurt or confused or a hundred other things that we all feel. He's a child. He needs love first."

Love first. The words plowed into his chest and knocked out what little wind he had. He'd watched her with her students. Her firm control still reflected love. She understood what a kid needed, and he knew that's what he lacked. The woman was a breathing compassion machine. If he only had half the concern and thoughtfulness she did. "I feel helpless, Molly. I've never said that to another human being."

"That's the first step to healing."

Healing? The doors began to close. She looked too deeply into his soul, and he didn't want her to dig up the dregs of his life. "I wondered if Randy is too young to take your class."

"He's not too young, but we only work with students in our school. Randy doesn't go there."

He knew that, but he'd hoped. "What

about private sessions?"

"Private?"

"School's out in less than two weeks. What about then?"

She looked at her latte and swirled the milky liquid.

Surprised at his bungle, he straightened in his seat. "I'd pay you, Molly. I didn't mean as a favor."

"Pay?" She eyed him, a thoughtful look growing on her face. "Do you own a dog?"

"A dog? I thought you would bring one."

Her shoulders fell, and she looked at him as if she were speaking to one of her students. "I can't pick up individual dogs for a client. The shelter brings them to the school. Anyway, it's not right for Randy. You want me to bring a dog for a lonely, confused boy to train and then take the dog away?" A deep breath poured from her lungs. "You can't do that to him. If you can't make the investment, then no one can."

"Investment?" Now she was talking about the building again. He knew it.

"Time. Investing your time."

He looked away, ashamed he'd misjudged her.

She didn't stop. "A dog adds a little work to your life, but you'll need one if you want me to help Randy."

She pushed the latte away from her. He'd lost interest, too.

"Think about what you're willing to do for the boy, and then I'll decide what I can do for you."

"But —"

She leaned in closer. "Brent, it's a good idea. I think you know what kind of companionship a dog can provide. They give people joy and friendship . . . and love. In my opinion, Randy needs all those things."

So do I. The words shot through Brent's mind like bullets. But a dog? He closed his eyes, envisioning the added confusion to his life, but then he thought of Randy. A dog would get him out of his room. The boy would have responsibilities. A playmate.

"If we get a dog, I will pay you for the training." From the look on her face, he knew her thoughts. "I can't promise you the building. I can recommend it, but it's up to the board of directors to approve such an unorthodox proposal."

"But you'll try?"

Her voice pleaded while his heart melted. "I'll need some things from you. I'd need a blueprint of what you want to do with the building. Since it would still be our property, the board will want to know that it will remain intact so it could be sold as a factory and offices someday."

"I can do that." Her hand raised to her chest as if she were holding back her heart.

"And we'll need some kind of plan of action. How you'll use the building, how you'll maintain it. They'll want to know everything."

Her face lit like the sun. "When would you need it?"

"I need it before I can approach them with the idea." She nodded before he finished.

"Give me a week, but I'll need to get inside the building again to measure and to calculate our needs."

"I can get someone to take you there." He fought back the desire to press his hand against hers. "Or I can take you."

Her face lit up. "What about tomorrow?"

He nodded, agreeing to what his heart told him to do. "That'll work. Can I bring Randy along? Maybe you can tell him about your program, and we'll see how he responds."

Her eyes questioned him as she leaned against the cushion. "You didn't talk to him about this yet?"

He lifted his hand in defense. "If he said yes, he'd be disappointed if you wouldn't agree. I didn't know how you'd respond."

From her look, she accepted his reasoning. "Yes, bring him along. I'd like to see him now that he's four years older. I'm sure he's changed. He must be about twelve?"

"Eleven, but he has a birthday in July."

Molly's tension seemed to vanish. "How about another coffee? One we'll actually drink."

"Great idea." He started to stand, but she extended her hand toward him.

"We have an agreement?"

Brent eyed her delicate fingers while his pulse jigged up his arm. "I agree to take your proposal to the board with your blueprint and your plan, and you agree to work with Randy."

"If you get a dog." A strained look stole to her face.

"If I get a dog."

"I know one that's available and needs training."

So did he.

CHAPTER SIX

The gate sat open and Molly spotted Brent's car near the side door to the building. She stepped onto the asphalt parking lot, slammed the door and hit the lock button on her key chain. She studied the building, shaken by the possibility that her dream might finally come true. If . . .

But she didn't want to think about the *if.* The board had to agree. She'd thought about it long and hard. She'd prayed, and her confidence had grown. An empty building was a tax deduction, but a building donated to a worthy cause was an additional write-off. They had to go for it.

She kicked a stone with the toe of her shoe as she headed toward the door, listening to the voices coming from inside. She recognized Brent's voice powering the conversation. Randy's soft tenor voice reached her ears as a hum. When she stepped inside, her shadow splayed across the floor, and Randy

125

spun around, followed by Brent's turn of the head.

His body followed. "You made it."

"Are you surprised?" She dug into her handbag and tugged out a hundred-foot tape measure, dropped her bag near the door and walked toward them.

Brent chuckled, motioning to the large tape. "You came prepared."

She noticed he had a smaller one clipped to his waistband. She grinned at him before focusing on Randy. "Remember me?"

The boy took a step back, his eyes shifting from Brent to her. Finally he nodded. "From school."

"You were in my class, but you've definitely grown up."

A faint grin stole across the boy's face, and he gave her a direct look for the first time.

She was taken aback by the same glinting eyes that Brent had, but the boy's were a softer blue, like a summer sky. Randy's past moody behavior, often charged with frustration, had altered. Today she witnessed a different boy, one who appeared shy and ill at ease.

Molly held out the tape measure. "Would you help me measure?"

He stood a moment as if weighing her offer. Finally he stepped closer and grasped the tape, then turned to Brent. "It's a bigger one than you have."

Brent laughed. "It sure is, but we'd better talk first before we measure anything."

A scowl tugged at her face. If he meant talk about their agreement, it meant he didn't trust her. "Talk about what?"

He held up his hand as if mollifying her attitude. "You need to decide what goes where. Do you want an office. A waiting room? A workroom? Cages? Indoor exercise space?"

She cringed. "Sorry. I thought —"

"I accept your apology." He grinned and headed for the front of the building. She followed.

When she looked behind her, Randy hadn't moved. Instead he'd yanked out the tape many feet and then, from his gleeful look, discovered the retraction button. He pushed it, and the tape came flinging back like a lizard's tongue and snapped back into the case. Randy's giggle resounded against the concrete walls.

"He's grown up."

Brent shifted. "I know."

Hearing the flack of Randy retracting the tape measure again, Molly moved closer to Brent. "He's a good-looking boy. His behavior isn't catching up to his age, either. Responsibility and a purpose would help him mature."

Brent's jaw tightened and a small muscle ticked in his cheek. His gaze shifted to Randy across the room, dragging out the tape again and flicking it back into its housing. "Let's talk about the building."

The smack of his words stung, but he was right. She'd stepped over the line and let her teacher persona slip beyond the bonds of their relationship. "I shouldn't have said that. It's not my business."

His neck circled her way and their eyes met. "I've made it your business, Molly, by asking you to help me. That's all I know to do right now."

The responsibility of Randy had obviously stretched Brent's ability to the max. He seemed like a lost puppy, searching for rescue. Molly stepped forward and rested her hand against his arm. "It'll come. Be yourself with him. He loves you, and that's what's important."

"Does he?" Doubt filled Brent's eyes.

"You know he does."

"Maybe I don't know the difference between love and tolerance, Molly."

She reeled from his comment but kept her expression steady. After meeting Brent's father, she couldn't imagine Brent's youth being that problematic. Molly's mind clicked with theories. What caused a man to lug around that kind of doubt in himself?

Realizing her hand still lay on his arm, she lifted her palm while the warmth of his skin continued coursing against her fingers. She rubbed her palm against her pant leg, needing to concentrate but being dragged away by the sensation.

"Let's get busy," she said, her voice too loud. She strode toward the entrance. "There's a room here in front. I think this will work fine for an office." She led him along, pointing to the area for a small lobby, a room for visitors to get to know a dog before adoption and a smaller room for ailing dogs.

As they walked, Randy darted toward them, his shyness less obvious. "What can I measure?"

"We're going to measure spaces for pens for the dogs." Molly pointed to the areas. "They'll be on both sides with a hallway down the middle."

Randy's eyes widened. "All the way to the back? That's a lot of dogs."

"Not all the way. We need a space for the dogs to play and another area for my partner's doggie day-care area."

"What's that?" Randy pulled out a stretch of tape and let it smack into the housing.

"A place people bring dogs when they work or go on vacation and can't be home with them. Like a child-care service."

Brent slipped behind her and rested his palms on her shoulders.

He surprised her. The sensation rolled down her chest and weakened her knees. He'd never touched her like that, though she'd longed for it to happen.

Brent drew in a lengthy breath. "Molly wants to have a shelter for dogs who don't have a home."

Randy's head lifted, and a frown wrinkled his smooth brow. "Like me."

Molly's chest tightened, and she grappled for a quick response. "Not really." Her fingers rolled into a fist, and she forced them apart. "You have family who loves you. These dogs have no one."

The boy shifted his gaze to Brent as silence filled the room. Molly closed her eyes, praying Brent would validate what she'd said. Brent's hands dropped from her shoulders, and she lifted her lids, hoping he would do the right thing.

Brent reached out and tousled Randy's hair. "We're buddies, aren't we?"

The boy tilted his head upward to look

into Brent's face, then nodded. He didn't seem to understand what was going on.

"Do you like dogs, Randy?" Molly asked.

He shrugged. "I've never had one."

"Really?" His response shouldn't have surprised Molly, but it had. "Every boy should own a dog." She noticed Brent's cheek tick again. "I have a program at the Montgomery Middle School called Teacher's Pet. My students help me train dogs to be obedient."

Randy's face brightened. "Really? Could I take your class?"

"You don't attend Montgomery Middle School, and it's for their students." She waved her hand. "But school's out in another week, and maybe we could work something out with your Uncle Brent."

He pivoted toward Brent like a child hearing the ice-cream man. "Could we?"

Brent winced, but he gave a slow nod. "We'll need to talk about it."

He shifted his focus to Molly, his eyes flashing a hidden message that she knew had to do with getting a dog. Her shoulders sank, hearing the sound in Brent's voice. She'd thought they'd made an agreement.

The boy's expression sank to a scowl. "Talk about what?"

Randy's question echoed Molly's.

131

"We would need a dog. You can't train a dog without owning one." Brent tilted his head, his eyes piercing his nephew's. "That means someone has to take care of it."

"I'll take care of him. I'll feed him and —"

"Clean the yard?" Brent's stern voice subsided. "That's the hard part."

Randy's nose wrinkled. "You mean . . ."

"Your uncle means clean up after the dog. It's not fun, but it's part of the responsibility of owning a pet and enjoying its company."

He thought a minute. "I can do that."

The boy's plaintive tone and Brent's earlier comment heightened Molly's awareness. Little by little she'd begun to piece Brent's problem together. As a boy, he'd made promises to his father he didn't keep, and the dog vanished. Ran away, Morris had told her. She wanted to know the full story.

Brent placed his hand on Randy's shoulder and looked into his eyes. "You promise?"

"I promise," Randy said. "Can we get a dog today?"

Brent drew back. "We have a job to do right now. Let's get busy."

"Let's measure." Randy tugged out the tape and handed Brent the end. "Where should we measure?"

Molly tried to calm her racing thoughts and pointed to the far wall. "How wide is this place? We need to know that first. Then we can decide about the size of the dogs' pens."

As Brent and Randy measured, Molly moved the puzzle pieces around her mind. Brent's problem had to do with caring for his pet, but it was more than that. It had to do with love and rejection, and she saw the same issues mirrored in Randy. She knew enough psychology to know the Runyan family had some serious relationship problems, but that wasn't hers to resolve. She'd come into his life for a dog shelter, and if she wanted to keep her dream alive, she needed to keep it that way.

Brent checked his watch and wiped his palms against his shirtsleeves. As soon as he thought about the appointment Molly had set with him, he'd broken into a sweat. He'd blamed his reaction on her shelter proposal, but he knew better. His efficient business tactics and shrewd dealings had died a silent death when it came to Molly. The woman had crept into his chest and was burrowing into his heart. Though he'd been in love once — he'd thought it was love — no other woman had affected him like Molly. She filled his mind and his dreams. He'd awaken at night, his heart palpitating like a man lost in a forest, a man fearing being eaten alive, yet loving the adventure.

He lowered his head in his hands, trying to deal with the new sensations that continued to weave through his chest.

"Headache?"

His head shot up, facing his fear head-on. "Molly. You're early."

"I took a half day off. I wanted to give the proposal a final edit." She strode across the room and dropped the folder on his desk. "I hope you think it's enough information for your board."

He rubbed his temples again, trying to get his mind on the proposal and not on the woman standing nearby.

"You do have a headache."

"I'm okay, Molly. Don't worry." He managed to get the words to leave his lips. "You said you needed a week, and here you are in four days."

A lighthearted tone filled her voice. "I had a proposal organized already. I just needed to tweak it. But before we talk, you should read it first," she said.

Brent saw no point trying to convince her. Molly didn't understand the word *no*. He'd watched her in action when it came to the building. Her determination and perseverance could win a blue ribbon at the fair. He opened the bound folder, paging through her purpose and mission statement, statistics on homeless dogs, the shelter's short- and long-range goals and plans, Teacher's Pet goals, cooperative organizations, support provided by the Oakland Pet Fund Organization, finances, funding and more.

"What do you think?" she asked.

He straightened his back and leaned forward. "I need to concentrate on this. Why not let me read it by myself, and if I find any problems, I'll let you know."

"I didn't mean to push you. I realize you're not feeling well."

"I'm fine. I just need —"

"To get a dog."

"Dog?" His neck tensed again. "Yes, I need to do that. Randy hasn't stopped asking."

"Then why not today?"

Like a guilty kid, he squirmed in the chair. "Because I'm working, and Randy's in school."

She glanced at her watch. "He'll be out shortly. It's nearly three."

Air drained from his lungs. "I doubt if they're open tonight."

"They're open until seven on Wednesday.

Today's Wednesday." The corner of her mouth lifted into a coy smile. "What do you say?"

Brent swiveled his head, amazed at her maneuvering. "Cornered."

She leaped from the edge of the desk. "Cornered? I thought I was being helpful."

She faked a pouty expression so flirtatious that it made his head spin. He'd never noticed Molly flirting before, and he couldn't win with that behavior. He had a hard time not buckling under to her determination. "I'll have to talk with Randy."

"Should I meet you there?"

Talking with Randy hadn't swayed her determination. She assumed Randy would be eager, and she assumed right. A dog. He pressed his fingers against his temple again.

"How about six? I'll meet you at the Humane Society."

He forced a nod.

Her expression softened. "You really need to do something about that headache."

"I will," he said, knowing his headache would soon be on her way.

Molly stood beside her car, and as soon as Brent's foot hit the brake, Randy darted from the passenger door before Brent could put it in Park.

136

Today his shyness had vanished, and he bounded toward her waving his arms. "I'm getting a dog."

Her stomach tightened seeing the boy's eagerness. Yet she knew kids, and they made promises that they didn't keep. How would Brent handle cleaning the yard and feeding the dog when the newness wore off? She hid her concerns and gave the boy a grin. "I know, and you promised to take care of the new dog, too."

He nodded. "Feed him and clean up . . . yuck." He gave her a crooked smile. "But I will."

"You'd better." Brent's voice cut into their conversation. He rested his hand on Randy's shoulder but looked at her. "You look chipper."

His tone sent a message, and she didn't doubt the meaning. "I'm happy for Randy." She thought a moment. "And for you. I know you enjoyed a dog when you were a boy."

Randy spun around. "You did? I thought you hated animals."

Brent flashed her a "button your lip" look, then shifted to Randy. "I had a dog once."

"You never told me." The boy's mouth drooped, and his eyes showed his hurt.

Molly gathered her thoughts to right her

mistake, but surprising her, Brent beat her to it.

"I'm sorry. I'll tell you about Toby later."

The name Toby caught in Brent's throat, and Molly's excitement twisted into anxiousness. She wanted a dog for the boy and for Brent, too. She hoped Randy would find a friend and something that would help him enjoy life, and she wanted to believe that Brent would heal from whatever happened in his past.

She lifted her shoulders above her concern. "Ready?" She glanced at her watch. "They close in forty minutes."

"I'm ready," Randy said, bounding in front of them toward the entrance.

When he was out of earshot, Molly clasped Brent's arm. "I didn't know you hadn't told him about owning a dog. I assumed —"

She felt him stiffen. "I should have. I'm a grown man acting like a kid. I need to get over it."

"Over what?"

He looked straight ahead. "It's nothing, Molly. The story is long and boring. I don't want to dig up all that old garbage. Not anymore."

It certainly wasn't boring. Nothing boring could affect a man like Brent had been affected. Whatever happened seemed to litter

138

his life with sadness and self-doubt. The controlled man she'd met weeks early had lost his armor. She had pried away his shield and somehow left him wounded.

Molly studied him as he opened the door to let Randy bounce in and then waited until she'd entered. Though he'd been hurt, she knew that wounds healed with good care and the proper treatment. Brent could be whole again. It would take time, and she needed patience and stamina. And she needed to face the truth. Brent didn't only represent the solution for the dog shelter. He meant so much more, and his pain had become hers. If she could learn to keep her mouth closed, she'd be a better friend.

"Molly."

The clerk's voice cut into her thoughts. "Hi, Kirk. We have an eager young man who wants to look for a dog."

Kirk motioned toward the kennel entrance. "You know where you're going." He looked at Randy. "You have lots of choices."

Molly moved ahead to the door while Randy paused and gave Kirk a thoughtful look. He turned toward Brent, then back to Kirk. "Me and my uncle will pick the best friend for us."

"Let's take a look." Molly pushed open the door. She observed Randy's face as he barreled alongside her, not wanting to miss a moment. She pulled open the next door, and the dogs' excitement filled the room.

Randy dashed from one cage to another while Brent stood at the threshold as if nailed there.

"Aren't you coming?"

"In a minute."

She strode away, heading for Randy and praying he'd notice the golden retriever. She stopped beside the boy as he knelt on the floor and petted the small dachshund she'd noticed on her last visit. Its long black nose and frankfurter body pressed against the wire, his long, thin tail beating against the floor.

"Do you like him?" Molly held her breath.

"He looks like a hot dog." He rose and looked down the row. "But I want a bigger dog."

Her lungs released pent-up air. "I noticed a really great dog here the other day." She guided him down the row, but he'd been diverted by a large black Lab. Ebony. The name had been attached to the door. "She's a girl."

Randy backed away. "A girl?"

Molly nodded. "Don't you like girls?"

"I want a boy dog."

Brent had appeared, and his frown melted

to a smile. "I'm not surprised. We boys stick together." His gaze shifted to Molly. "But girls are nice, too."

"Yuck." Randy shook his head.

She chuckled, but Brent stood a moment, his gaze riveted to hers, letting her know the girl comment was meant for her. Molly's pulse skipped like kids heading out for recess. "We'd better get moving before they close."

Brent blinked as if unaware he'd been staring. He spun around and headed down the row of pens, and when he slowed, Molly knew he had neared Rocket.

She edged her way closer as he crouched beside the dog and petted his nose through the barricade.

"Is he a boy?"

Randy's question jarred the tender moment. "He's a boy. His name's Rocket." She turned over the information sheet and looked on the back. "He's three years old."

"Rocket." Randy nestled down beside Brent and let the golden retriever lick his fingers. "He likes me."

"He does," Brent said, his voice sounding tight. He lowered his hand from the cage and stepped back.

Randy stood, too, and continued down the row, stopping to pet another dog.

Molly watched Brent's expression, trying to decide if Brent wanted Randy to choose Rocket or a dog that wouldn't remind him of Toby, who'd been a symbol of the love that should have been in his life. She knew it, and she suspected Brent did, too. The dog might cause too much pain for him.

"Is this one a boy?"

Molly strode forward and eyed the dog — a black-and-white setter. She flipped over the card. She didn't want to tell him the truth. "He's a boy. He's five."

"What's his name?"

She pointed to the sign.

"Rascal." He withdrew his focus from the name card and gazed down the aisle toward Brent. "Do you like this one?"

Brent sauntered toward them and glanced into the pen. "It's your dog, so it's your decision."

Randy studied the setter. "I know which one I want."

A vise clenched Molly's heart. "Are you sure?"

Randy nodded and then turned and whipped past them. "Rocket loves me, and I love him." He swung around to face Brent. "Can I have Rocket?"

Brent looked as if the weight of the world plunged from his shoulders. His head shot upward and his stride picked up speed. "If you're sure, I think he's a good choice."

"Yep. That's the dog I want."

Molly viewed the two smiling faces, and her heart danced a jig.

CHAPTER SEVEN

"Randy, what are you doing?"

The boy stood over the dog's bowl pouring dry dog food that fell to the kitchen floor. "I'm feeding Rocky."

Brent managed to calm his voice. "The bowl is full. You just fed him this morning."

"But he's hungry. He keeps watching me eat my sandwich."

Brent dragged out a sigh and headed for the closet. "Please clean up that food." He handed Randy the broom and dustpan. "Dogs beg. They're not hungry. They just want what you have. That's something you need to learn."

"He looks hungry."

Brent held up his hand. "We feed him once a day and keep his water filled." He gave his nephew a piercing stare. "Do you understand?"

Randy didn't respond. He swept the nuggets, flinging them farther onto the kitchen

144

floor while Rocket bounded after the food. It became a game that revved Brent's patience. He grabbed the broom from Randy's hand. "Look. We can take the dog back if . . ."

The look on Randy's face stopped him cold. What was he doing? Memories crashed over him. Dogs and kids took patience. He'd experienced the lack of understanding in his father. Do it his way or no way . . . while his brother taunted him from the sidelines.

When Brent realized Randy's problem, shame weighted his shoulders. "Have you ever used a broom?"

Randy shook his head as the words *learn to be a dad* filled his mind.

Rocket sprinted around the kitchen gobbling up the dry pellets, and if he didn't act, the food would vanish before they cleaned it up.

Brent spun around and faced the dog. "Rocket. No." He pinpointed the retriever with his index finger. The dog eyed him, then the food, then him again. "Sit."

Rocket sat. Relief washed over Brent. Okay. He'd experienced one moment of success. Now Randy. "I'll show you how to sweep."

He demonstrated while Randy watched

and then gave him back the broom and watched him pull what nuggets were left into a pile.

"Now, hold the dustpan like this." Brent bent down and showed him how to guide the pellets into the scoop. "Now you do it."

Randy followed his example and looked at him with a grin. "Like this?"

He smiled back. "Great job." He tousled Randy's hair and lifted the trash lid for him to toss the nuggets. "We need to work together to make Rocket healthy. He can't eat too much or he'll get fat and sick."

Randy turned his back and crossed the room. Brent jammed his fists into his waist, irked by Randy's rudeness. When he realized Randy was returning the items to the closet, Brent lowered his arms, cautioning himself to be more tolerant. Randy's hyper behavior took understanding, and that's what happened when he became excited.

Brent could relate. His own behavior hadn't been normal since meeting Molly.

Randy came bounding back with Rocket at his side, his eyes glinting. "If Rocky's too fat, he wouldn't play with me."

"That's right." Brent drew in a breath. Randy did understand. Maybe he and Randy could both change for the better. He did a double take. "What's this Rocky stuff?"

Randy gave him sly smile. "When you're mad at me, you call me Randall, so I thought —"

"You'd call him Rocket when he's bad and Rocky when he's good." Brent chuckled.

Randy's playful grin grew.

Brent opened his arms and wrapped them around the boy. His stomach tightened as he felt Randy's slender frame in his arms. When was the last time anyone had hugged the boy? Brent's mind segued back to his childhood. He'd longed to be hugged by his father, and it never happened. Though Brent's mother had been more affectionate, she followed his father's rule that boys needed to be strong and not treated like babies. Brent had been treated like a man as far back as he could remember. He gave Randy a final squeeze. The boy needed lots of hugs.

The telephone's jingle broke into his thoughts. He unwrapped his arms from Randy and grabbed the receiver from the wall phone. His chest pulsed when he heard Molly's voice. "What's up?"

"I just wondered how you're doing with the dog."

He heard an undertone in her voice.

147

"Fairly well. We're both learning some lessons." He glanced at Randy, sitting at the kitchen table beside his half-eaten sandwich petting Rocket. He needed to break the dog's habit of begging at the table.

Molly's voice intruded on his thoughts. "Lessons? I hope you're not having —"

"No problems, really. In fact, I was surprised to see that he obeyed when I said no."

"Randy or the dog?"

He chuckled. "Both, actually." He glanced at Randy again as he reached for his sandwich. "Wash your hands before you pick up food."

Randy glanced at the dog and his hands and then rose and headed for the sink.

The line lay silent except for her breathing.

"Sorry. We had a little overfeeding-the-dog mishap today."

"Do you need some help, Brent? I'd be glad to come over."

Come over. His lungs worked harder. What did that woman do to him? He'd spent his lifetime controlling his emotions, but somewhere along the line he'd lost it. A man demanded control. He clutched the phone and held his breath. "Did you want to start the lessons today? I know Randy's finished with school, but I thought you wanted to wait until school's closed for the summer."

"I'm finished next Wednesday, but today's Saturday. I'm free."

Brent hadn't prayed in years, but he felt himself wishing that he could ask God what to do. He could deny his feelings, but who would he be fooling? Getting involved with anyone wouldn't work. Dating led to expectations. Not just Molly's but his own. He'd closed himself off too tightly to be a good companion, especially a husband, and he scuffled to be a father figure to Randy.

Brent drew in a lengthy breath. "Probably not today, but thanks."

Seconds ticked by with only silence. "I only wanted to help. I know I finagled you into getting a dog, and I feel guilty."

"Don't feel guilty. I'm the one who asked about the Teacher's Pet program." He wished he could drag the words back. He gazed across the room and saw Randy's gaze bearing down on him as he listened.

"Is that Molly?"

"Hang on," he said as he covered the receiver. "Yes, she offered to come for your first obedience lesson with the dog."

"Obedience?"

"You know. Training Rocket to behave."

"I remember." His face filled with anticipation. "Is she coming?"

His heart skipped. His purpose for adopting the dog was for Randy to have responsibility and purpose. Being a father meant following through on his promises, and he couldn't hide from Molly the rest of his life. He needed to be strong. He couldn't let her turn him into mush every time he saw her.

"Have her come today." His expression grew to a grin. "Please."

Please. How long had it been since that word crossed Randy's lips? Brent lifted his hand from the receiver. For Randy's sake, he had to deal with his emotions.

Randy and Rocket were waiting in the front yard when Molly pulled up. She eyed the house a moment, admiring the stately brick colonial with its multitude of windows opening the rooms to sunlight. She hopped out of the car carrying a dog collar in case Brent had purchased a choke chain. She didn't approve of those. A stern voice and reward for obedience motivated a dog without hurting him. That's all a trainer needed.

"Hi," she said, rounding the car and striding up the brick sidewalk. She could imagine the beauty of the landscape if Brent had added some flowers, but the shrubs were neat and well trimmed.

"Are you ready for your first lesson?" She eyed the doorway, then the window, hoping to see Brent. No such luck.

Randy appeared shy today, as his eyes drifted from her to the dog. "We have a collar." He grasped the dog's neck and pulled it upward so she could see it.

Molly was pleased to see one like her own. "Do you have a leash?"

He nodded. "It's in the house."

"Let's go into the backyard. There's less distractions there." She grasped Rocket's collar. "Go inside and get the leash while I take him around."

When Randy had vanished inside, Molly let go, and the dog followed her to the back gate. From her experience as a trainer, she figured the dog would be easy to teach. She opened the gate and stepped into the lovely backyard. Again no flowers, but a birdbath and a bench sat in the far corner surrounded by low-lying shrubbery. Pines and maples dotted the periphery. She also noted the lack of entertainment for Randy. No basketball hoop on the garage. No horseshoe pit, and there was plenty of room.

Randy came barreling through the doorway with the leash. He reached her before she could pull her gaze from the doorway, hoping to see Brent follow. He didn't appear. Disappointed, she glanced at Randy beside her with the leash in his hand, a questioning look on his face.

"Let's get started." She found the ring on Rocket's collar. "Hook the leash." Randy did as she said, and she handed it to him. "Your uncle said Rocket seemed to understand the meaning of 'sit.' So let's practice that first. He needs to know 'sit' before other commands." She dug into the pocket of her jeans and pulled out a bag of dog nuggets. "We use these as a reward."

When Rocket smelled the food, he bounded around her feet and tangled Randy in the leash.

Molly unknotted the strap and gave it back to Randy. "Never give him even one nugget when he disobeys. That's important."

Randy agreed and began to practice what she'd demonstrated.

While he practiced, Molly eyed the doorway again, then jerked her head away, chastising herself. Why moon over someone who wouldn't make a perfect partner? The answer followed immediately: because he'd captured her interest. He'd drag out feelings she'd forced to lay dormant.

Molly didn't know if she could trust

herself. When she'd been a teen, she'd led a life she didn't want to admit, one that shamed her to this day. She went against all that her parents had taught her and all that God expected. The parties with no parents home, the drinking and the backseats of cars. Molly hated the memories. If she married, she wanted a Christian, but how could she tell a Christian how far she'd strayed from her beliefs?

Pulling her mind to the present, she focused on Randy. "Good job." She gave him a broad smile, touched by the excitement in his face.

Molly's parents filled her mind. A perfect couple. A perfect marriage. Her two siblings had failed marriages. She didn't want that. Emotions played tricks, and she didn't want to make more mistakes, not when it came to what the Bible said. The Lord wanted marriage to be for life. She couldn't chance following in her siblings' footsteps, and she had no guarantee with the bad choices she'd made in her past. Best to ignore those sensations she felt with Brent. She knew what they meant, and she wanted no part of promiscuity. Never again, and she sensed Brent wanted no part of marriage.

The words no more than struck her when the door opened and Brent stepped outside.

Despite the talking-to she'd given herself moments earlier, her sensations hadn't listened. She was breathless.

He stood still and watched Randy.

She regarded the boy. "I think we're ready for the 'stay' command."

His head shot upward as eagerness danced in his eyes. "What do I do?"

"Do you still have nuggets?"

He showed her the baggy.

Rocket lifted his haunches to rise but then had second thoughts. Good dog.

"I'll show you the first time." Molly reached into the bag for a couple of dog pellets. "I'm going to get him to sit and give him one pellet, and then watch what I do next."

As she began to work with Rocket, Brent moved closer and stood beside Randy. "It won't hurt you to learn this, too," she said to Brent, as she used her empty hand like a stop sign in front of Rocket's nose. She backed up a few steps, keeping the dog in focus. "Stay." She remained in place and waited.

He gave a little whimper but stayed. She gave him a nugget and backed up farther and waited a few moments before she said "come" with as much enthusiasm she could muster under the circumstances.

Rocket darted her way. "Good boy," she said, giving him the treat. "Just keep in mind that dogs learn to obey if they trust you. They will follow your lead unless it goes against their nature." She turned to Randy. "Dogs don't look at the outside of people — they can look in their hearts. That's what they trust." She gave Randy a pat. "Now it's your turn, and then your uncle's."

"Not me." Brent backed away. "He's Randy's dog."

Molly saw the love in Brent's eyes when he looked at the beautiful golden retriever. She could only imagine when he was a child what it had been like to lose his pet. She swallowed and forced herself to keep her mouth shut.

Brent planted his feet apart and watched Randy while Molly kept her eye on Rocket, but she sensed Brent's nearness. "When I called here earlier I had another reason for calling." She kept her voice soft.

"Another reason?"

She tilted her head. Could he be so dumb? "The proposal. I wondered about the status."

Brent looked dazed for a moment. "The board has copies. I e-mailed it to them for our next meeting."

She opened her mouth to ask.

"Monday. I should know something Monday."

Anticipating the board's decision made her eager for Monday, but Brent was definitely avoiding her for some reason. He kept his focus on Randy, his arms folded across his chest like a barricade.

"I'm sorry I made you feel you had to invite me today, Brent." He finally looked at her. "We'll be done soon, and I'll be out of here."

His gaze lowered. "Don't apologize. Randy needs to work with the dog. It's not you, Molly. It's me."

"It's you? What does that mean?"

"I'm not used to people in my life. I'm trying to adjust to Randy, and now . . ."

He seemed unnerved, and Molly struggled to make sense out of what he was trying to say.

Brent shifted from one foot to the other. "I'm not good at relationships."

Relationships? She studied him a moment. "Don't you have friends?"

"Not many. I suppose I'm like Randy — or I should say he's like me. I'm a loner."

"That's too bad."

His head snapped upward, and he looked disturbed.

"Friendships are important. You both

need them. And it can't just be a dog. I know the saying 'A dog's man's best friend,' but we all need human contact."

"Maybe some people don't."

"You mean some people can't open their hearts wide enough to let people in." She captured his gaze. "Work on it, Brent. Randy needs you."

And so do I. The thought fell into her head before she could stop it.

"Come, Fred." Molly clapped her hands and watched Fred run the other way deeper into the park. "Steph, I'm not kidding. When we get the shelter, you need to know how to work with the dogs, or you'll undo what I'm trying to accomplish."

Steph gave a grunt. "I know."

"Are you practicing?"

"I'm not one of your middle-schoolers, Molly." She punched her fists into her hips. "I thought you wanted to get together to talk about the shelter."

Molly straightened. "That's true, but I also wanted to keep busy. I'm nervous."

Steph moved closer. "Nervous about what?"

Fred joined the twosome, sniffing around Molly's feet as if she'd stepped on a hunk of steak. "Sit." To her surprise, the dog did.

Her eyebrows lifted. "Good job, Steph."

"Thanks. I did work on that one." Steph scratched Fred's head. "Nervous about what?"

"Today's the day."

"You mean when you'll know for sure about the proposal?"

Molly nodded, the lump in her throat constricting her ability to talk.

Steph gave her a questioning look. "Are you going to cry?" She grasped Molly's shoulder. "I've never seen you cry. Never."

"I'm fine." She brushed the moisture from her eyes, frustrated that she'd allowed her emotions to get so out of control. "This means so much to me . . . to us. The perfect place for the dogs and for your day care. Perfect." The tears pooled, and she swiped at them again. "It's my dream."

Steph wrapped her arms around her shoulders. "I know, but if this doesn't pan out, it's not the end. You'll have other opportunities."

Molly pulled away. "Don't even say that. I'm standing on the brink of a miracle, and you're trying to push me over the cliff."

"I am not." Steph gave her an angry stare. "I'm your friend and want this, too, but we need to accept failure and success. I'm worried about funding this anyway. The pittance

158

I contributed won't make a dent in what you need, especially with the building renovations."

"We'll manage, and you're donating your time." She lowered her eyes, wishing she could give Steph a small salary for helping to run the shelter during the day. "I'll still be teaching in the fall, and we'll have money coming in from the adoption donations and from the obedience training classes."

"I hope you know what you're doing."

Molly bit her tongue rather than snap another response and folded her arms. "It'll be a success, Steph, and once the shelter's stable and bringing in some income, I'll be there full-time. And once we have the building, you can take in more dogs for your day care. You can quit your part-time job." She glanced at her watch and then walked away and returned, trying not to trip over Fred. "Steph, he's not going to call."

"Wearing a path in the grass isn't going to help. Brent called before. Why not today?"

"Because it's bad news." Molly pulled out her cell phone and peered at the screen. "Nothing. No text. No missed call." She checked her volume. High. She shoved it back into her pocket. Taking her frustrations out on her friend made no sense. She opened her arms. "Sorry. I'm just edgy. *A man's wisdom gives him patience."*

Steph walked into her embrace and gave her a hug. "I suppose that's from the Bible."

Once again, Molly kept her mouth closed. She wanted to comment that if Steph would go to church or even read a Bible she would know it was from Scripture. She tightened her hug, praying the Lord would open Steph's heart to His Word. She prayed the same prayer for Brent.

"But that's not the only thing bothering you, is it?"

Molly's head jerked upward. "What do you mean?" She could never fool Steph.

She folded her arms across her chest. "Mama Steph is waiting. Tell all."

Molly walked away, hoping to drop the subject.

"I know this is as much about Brent as the building. He's ignoring you? You have a thing for him. I've never seen you fall for someone before like you have him."

"I have not 'fallen' for him."

"Okay. What do you call it?"

"He's a friend." She wondered about that even. "An acquaintance."

"Acquaintance? You're crazy about him."

"I'm just crazy, Steph." She massaged her forehead to hold back a headache. "I've never gotten involved with anyone. I want a

160

solid marriage like my parents, one that's pleasing to God." Molly swallowed her desire to tell Steph about her past mistakes, but telling her wouldn't get rid of the sadness any more than knowing God had forgiven her. She needed to forgive herself. "Steph, you know how I feel about getting involved. I can't take a chance, especially with Brent. He has problems of his own."

"Tell that to your heart, Molly."

Though Molly could deny it until she turned pink, her friend had dragged out the truth. "What do I do now?"

The silence was broken by the her ring tone jingling "How Much Is That Doggie in the Window?"

"First, I think you should answer your cell phone."

Molly grasped the phone from her pocket. Brent's name popped into the window while nausea rolled through her stomach. "It's him."

"Then answer it," Steph said, rolling her eyes.

Molly flipped open the phone. The moment she heard his voice she knew.

"I'm sorry, Molly, but it's not over. They want more details. They asked for more funding information. They want to know everything. They're worried you'll make a mess of it and then walk away."

"I wouldn't do that." Her voice came out as a whisper.

"I know that, but they don't. They want to check on the tax status information. They're talking to our CPA and legal people. They're suspicious."

"Suspicious?" A frown carved her face. "Of me?"

"They don't know you."

"Didn't you tell them?"

Silence.

"Brent." Her fist clenched against her chest. "Didn't you tell them how well you know me?"

"My personal business isn't theirs. They'll misconstrue it."

"What do you mean?"

"I — I . . . I don't have women in my life, Molly. I told you that, and they'd think I'd fallen head over heels and lost my mind."

Her body tensed. "I don't want head over heels, Brent, but I'd hoped by now you would consider me a friend."

"Molly."

In the silence following her name, she waited as tension built.

"You came into my life in a strange way, Molly. I don't know how to explain it. You've become a . . . sort of a —"

She swiped at her eyes again. "Never mind, Brent. I understand. Just make a list of what they want and e-mail it."

"E-mail?"

"Yes. E-mail." She closed her eyes. "Thanks for trying."

"Molly, please, I —"

"I'm busy right now, Brent. Just send me a list of what you need, and I'll see what I can do." She closed the phone before any more was said. *Sort of.* Sort of what? What was she to him? A headache. That's what she was. A big fat pain in the neck. A huge sliver in his finger. No one wanted a sliver. They did what they could to get rid of it.

She spun around. "Let's work with Fred."

Steph's jaw drooped. "Molly, what happened?"

"Nothing."

Steph grasped her arm and drew her closer.

Molly jerked away. "They want more information."

"What kind of information?

"It doesn't matter. Funding guarantees. They think I'm out to rip them off."

Steph shook her head. "You're disappointed."

"No, I'm furious."

Steph opened her arms. "I told you not to —"

"I know. You told me so. Now let's talk about something else."

Steph closed her eyes. "Fred needs to learn the meaning of 'stay.' Let's do that."

Molly gnawed her lip. She'd not only attacked Brent, but now she'd yelled at her best friend. She needed to slow down, to practice patience, and she needed to be thankful. She'd spent her life being independent and evaded the whole romance thing. Relationships were restricting and too much work. Brent was doing her a favor.

Her head swam as hope sank to the pit of her stomach.

CHAPTER EIGHT

Brent sat in an easy chair in his great room, watching Randy and Rocket through the window. Molly had been right. Randy had finally come out of his bedroom. And out of his shell. They talked now, and Randy laughed more than he'd ever heard in the past. The look on his face touched Brent with a quiet kind of happiness, maybe comfort, that he'd never felt.

His deepest sadness now was Molly. He hadn't been honest with her. She wasn't sort of a friend. She was so much more. He'd heard her deflate like a punctured balloon. She'd opened his eyes to so many things, so what did he fear? She could open doors, doors he'd nailed closed . . . or tried to.

He lowered his head, knowing he'd failed. Now what? He'd walked to the phone three times since he got home from work to apologize, but he'd pulled his hand away, wanting to make a clean cut with Molly.

Leading her on wasn't fair. Clean cut? What he'd done had been a jagged slash that had hurt them both.

For the first time in his life, he sensed someone really cared about him. With all her bravado and spirit, he'd seen her heart filled with love and concern for others, a tenderness he'd never known, not even from his mother.

Though his mother had been a good woman, she'd marched under his father's baton. Their church had been her priority, and the social clubs, important to his father, had also taken her time. Even then she struggled to make a good home but one that didn't include sitting on the floor to play games with him or to read him a story at night.

Get over it. He slapped his hand against the chair arm. How long did he plan to drag around the old baggage? He knew the Bible said to lay his burdens at Jesus' feet, but he'd felt rejected by the Lord, too. More than rejected. Punished.

Forgiveness. The word slammed into his defenses. What had Molly said about dogs? They gave unconditional love. They forgave before a person did anything. Isn't that what God had done? He'd sent his son to wipe away sins before they even happened. He'd watched his faith flail like a drowning man in a stormy sea, and he ignored the life raft God had sent to save him.

Molly had said dogs always obeyed unless it went against nature. That was his problem. Too many things went against his nature. And Molly seemed to know. Her voice filled Brent's mind. *Dogs don't look at you on the outside. They look in your heart.* Is that what she'd done? Looked into his heart and thought he was worth saving?

He wrenched himself from his thoughts and strode to the window to watch Randy. The boy needed a real dad, not an uncle learning to be one. And if he were a good uncle, he'd go outside and play with them, but —

Before he could give an excuse, Randy and Rocket bolted past the window as if a circus parade had come down the street.

Curious, Brent headed for the foyer. He flung open the front door, half hoping Molly had come to surprise him. Instead he saw his father bending over to pet Toby . . . Rocket. His heart felt full. He pulled open the front door and stepped onto the brick porch. "Dad. What are you doing here?"

His father glanced his way, gave Rocket a final pat, then strode toward him. "I was in the area and thought I'd see how things are going."

Brent didn't believe him. He ambled down the steps to the sidewalk. "You've met Rocket, I see."

His father's eyes searched his face before he nodded. "He's a good-looking dog." He tucked his hands into his pants pockets. "I can't help but think of Toby."

Memories charged through Brent. "He was Randy's choice, not mine."

His father didn't respond.

"Grandpa," Randy called and bounded to his side with Rocket whipping past them to chase a squirrel. "Will you play with us? I can show you what Rocky can do. He can sit and stay and come when I tell him."

Brent's dad rested his hand on Randy's head and pivoted it toward Brent. "That's probably better behavior than you have." He gave his grandson a smile.

"I'm really good, Grandpa. You can ask Uncle Brent."

Brent nodded his head, and Randy flashed a grin and then darted after Rocket. Brent followed him with his gaze, knowing his father never dropped in for a visit without a motive. "Come in, Dad. I'll make us some coffee." He turned to Randy, running in circles with the dog. "When you're through playing, don't forget to clean the yard. That's why you came out."

"I know," he said, his eagerness taking a nosedive.

Brent climbed the four steps and held the door open for his father. He took a shortcut through the dining room to the kitchen, his dad following.

"You can sit in the great room if you'd like. I'll be there in a minute."

"This is fine." His father walked past the island and pulled out a chair from beneath the breakfast-room table. When he sat, he leaned back and folded his hands.

Brent's gaze darted from the coffeemaker to his father, anticipating what might come next. He hit the on button and joined his dad at the table. The water gurgled into the pot, already sending out the brisk scent of the strong Columbian blend.

"What's on your mind, Dad?"

His father's knitted fingers flexed. "Do I have to have something on my mind?"

"You don't drop by for a visit very often for no reason."

"I appreciate your taking Randy, Brent, and I want you to know that." He glanced out the window and watched Rocket wander along with Randy as he cleaned the yard.

"He looks happier than I've seen him in a

long time," his dad said.

"I've noticed. It's the dog, not me."

His father gave him a thoughtful look. "I'm sure it's both. Seeing the dog takes me back. I did you a disservice when you were a boy." His index fingers bounced against each other. "I'm sorry about that." His head lowered again. "I know it's too late now, but —"

Brent's breath hitched. "No, it's not, Dad."

His dad's eyes flashed upward. "But I made a mess of things. Your brother always dominated our lives, and you just shrank away after that."

"You told me a lie, and it hurt."

A deep frown wrinkled his father's forehead. "Lie? What do you mean?" He sank into the nearest chair.

"You told me Toby had run away during the hunting trip. I suppose I knew better than that, but I accepted it. You're my dad, and I believed you."

His father's head drooped. "I didn't have the courage to tell you the truth. I was upset with you and . . . I shouldn't have lied. That was very wrong. I needed to be man enough to tell you I gave the dog away. I suppose your brother told you the truth."

The memory seared through Brent. "In

great detail with a smile."

"He was like that for some reason. I didn't know." He unknotted his fingers and reached across the table, his veined hands pressing against Brent's.

"Dad, you have no idea what thoughts went through my mind. I couldn't imagine Toby running away, and so I thought . . ." He struggled to get the words out. "I thought Randall shot him."

His father's eyes flew upon. "Shot Toby?"

Brent's heart thundered against his chest. "On purpose." He drew in a lengthy breath. "That's what I thought."

"Brent. No." He dropped his face into his hands. "I had no idea you would think something like that. I'm so sorry." He lowered his hands, his face mottled.

Brent wished he'd never spoken the words. "I was a lonely boy. Naturally when I got older I realized the idea was foolish."

His father shook his head. "You had every right to think the worst. I know how Randall taunted you. I hoped you would learn to be stronger." He lowered his head. "The first mistake was to give Toby away. He was a good dog, and you were a boy. The second was not telling you the truth."

Brent closed his eyes, clinging to his father's apology like a gift.

His dad rose again and ambled toward the window. "That's why I was afraid to raise Randy. I'd made so many mistakes with you and your brother, and I didn't want to do that again. I'm not a good father. I don't know how to fix that."

"You've just started."

He gave Brent a thoughtful look. "I suppose I have."

The gurgling had halted, and Brent rose and prepared two mugs of coffee, both black — the way he and his father liked it. He set a mug in front of his dad and sat and took a sip of his drink. The brisk taste calmed him.

His dad eyed the steam and then took a careful sip. "That's good stuff." He set the mug back on the table. "You know, Brent, I'm proud of you. I don't suppose I've ever told you that."

Brent's chest tightened. "No, you haven't."

"And you're perceptive."

"Perceptive?"

"I did have another reason for coming here."

Brent grinned. "It was just a guess."

"No, it's the way you look at people. You can see inside them." He pursed his lips. "I've been thinking about the young woman with the dog-shelter proposal." He pinpointed Brent with his eyes. "Molly."

Brent's knee jerked. He'd been thinking about her, too, continuously. "What about her?"

"I like her. She's discerning and determined with brains behind it, and she has a good heart."

Brent averted his eyes. If he didn't, his father would read too much. "She is determined, I'll agree with that."

"I like a woman with drive and spunk. Your mom didn't have that, but she was a good and faithful wife. She did everything for me." His expression pinched. "That was a mistake I should have stopped, too. She should have given you boys more."

Brent couldn't handle the family diagnostics. "So what about Molly?"

"You didn't let me know about the board's decision. They agreed with her proposal, I'm sure."

Brent drew in a lengthy breath. "Not exactly."

His father straightened. "What's the problem?"

"Funding. They want to know where she'll get the money to renovate the building for their needs and then pay the bills. She's using her savings, and a friend's pitching in a small amount. She'll share the space with a doggie day care."

"That's all they have?"

"Until they start bringing in money from the adoptions and her dog obedience training."

"But that takes time." A scowl grew on his father's face.

"I know, but she said she'd see what she could do. Once she gives me the answers to their questions, it'll go for a vote."

"When's that?"

"They want to finish with the proposal next Monday. That doesn't give her much time."

His father rose. "No, it doesn't." He took a final drink of his coffee and slid the chair against the table. "I need to go, Brent. Thanks for the coffee, and for the talk. I should have said these things years ago."

Brent rose and extended his hand. "It's still good to hear, Dad. Thanks."

Instead of grasping Brent's hands, his father moved toward him and opened his arms. Brent froze for a moment, never having received an embrace from him. He shrugged off his discomfort and accepted it. His father's musky aftershave was oddly comforting. He'd worn that fragrance since Brent could remember.

His father said goodbye to Randy and Rocket, and Brent walked him to the car.

As he pulled away, Brent's emotions plowed over him. He shook his head as he strode into the house, overwhelmed by what had occurred. His father was proud of him. He sank into the kitchen chair, staring at his coffee mug.

Forgiveness. In God's time. He remembered his mother's pet phrase when he and Randall wanted something right then. "All good things happen in God's time, boys. Be patient." Today those words had a new meaning.

He bolted from the chair and grasped the wall phone, punched in Molly's telephone number and waited. He wasn't sure what he was going to say, but he needed to hear her voice.

"Molly," he said, when she answered, "how are the revisions going?"

She hemmed a moment as if he'd surprised her. "Slow."

Slow. Her discouragement resounded in that single word. "Can I do anything?"

"Not really."

"Molly, I'm sorry if I sounded distracted the last time you were over. I've had a lot on my mind." For one, she'd been there. Always. He wiped the perspiration from his palm. "But that's no excuse. I am your friend, and I want this proposal to succeed, so let me help in any way I can."

The line went silent a moment.

"Molly?"

"I'm thinking, Brent. I'm okay, and thanks for your offer and the apology, but I need to do this by myself. I've had a few additions. A year's supply of dog food, donated by a pet store. A veterinarian I know is willing to volunteer two hours one Saturday a month to give the dogs their shots and physical checkups, but I'll need more from a vet than that. At least at first."

"I could make calls."

"They don't know you."

"Could I come over? I'd have to bring Randy, but —"

"No. Thanks. Really, I need to do this myself. I'll give you what I can in a couple of days."

"If you're sure."

She didn't answer, and he finally said goodbye, wishing he'd been more open from the beginning. His dad had been right. Molly's determination and intelligence couldn't be questioned. And her loving heart. He'd damaged it, he was certain.

Molly reviewed the additional information she had ready for Brent and then placed it into a folder and set it on her desk. She eyed it, wanting to call him to see if she could hand deliver it to his house. Instead she decided to e-mail it.

Bite your nose to spite your face. How many times had her mother warned her of that?

Her mother. Her parents were the modern-day Cleavers, June and Ward. Their relationship served as her model of what married life should be like, and her parents had come through, beyond her expectations. She'd asked them for financial help for the shelter, and they'd promised a monthly stipend until the business was self-sufficient. Though it was, by far, not all she needed, the donation gave her hope. Her dad had even volunteered to come to Michigan to help get the building ready for business. They behaved as their strong faith required. A faith stronger than hers seemed to be. Though she prayed for guidance, she feared the Lord might take her down a path she didn't want to go.

Pulling up her shoulders, she grasped the folder and marched to her computer to e-mail Brent the information. She glanced at her watch. He'd still be at work, so he'd get it today. After she'd sent the information, she settled into her favorite chair, trying to make sense out of her life.

Wednesday she'd finished the grade reports, turned in the books and cleaned her classroom. Today she was officially on vacation. She loved the free time, but this year her mind felt bogged down with so many things, things that should be wonderful, but left her fearful, too. The building proposal could fail, and that meant starting again. She'd have to find another building and begin a new negotiation. Her means — even with her parent's commitment and Steph's — didn't cover the cost of renting a building.

Then Brent. What did she want? A friendship for sure. She would miss his amazing dark blue eyes that often filled her dreams. She would miss Randy and Rocket. She would miss the hope of ever falling in love. No man had stirred her as Brent had done. He charged her with sensations she couldn't explain — excitement, confusion, hope. Hope? Had he really given her hope?

The answer was yes. Hope for the shelter and hope for a life that included more than her own plans and dreams. She drew back as a scowl settled on her face. Did Brent have a dream? He seemed on the edge of an abyss, and he certainly wouldn't be dreaming of falling over. Could his dream be to step away from everything to find himself?

Molly rolled back her computer chair and headed into the kitchen. She opened the refrigerator and pulled out a pitcher of unsweetened iced tea. She filled a glass and popped in a slice of frozen lemon and a few ice cubes. She liked her drink cold. The first brisk taste brightened her spirit, and she headed into the living room. The sun shone through the window, beckoning her outside, but to what? She didn't have a yard like Brent's. No gazebo to sit in and enjoy a breeze or watch bunnies hop through the grass. She looked out on the parking lot or the side of another condo.

Still it was home. She looked around the empty space. If only she had a dog.

The telephone rang. She uncurled her legs and grasped the remote. Brent's voice charged through her, and once again she caught her breath while thoughts became words. "Did you get the information?"

"Yes, thanks. I haven't digested it yet, but I thought maybe . . ."

He paused and Molly hung on his words.

"Maybe you'd like to discuss it face-to-face. I could come there. Randy's at my dad's for the night. Or better yet, you could come here for dinner. I'll make you one of my specialties."

At this point, Molly didn't care about his

specialty. She longed to see him — the way they'd been when they talked and joked. She missed that. A sweet longing twined through her mind until a new thought poisoned the bright tendrils. "Do you want to see me because of a problem? Is there something wrong with what I sent?"

"No. That's not it. I've only skimmed it, but I'll read it before I get home. Could you come about six? We can talk about it then."

Concern prickled up her arms, but the dinner invitation was a good sign. "I'll see you at six."

"Nothing fancy, okay?"

"I'll leave my ball gown at home."

He chuckled, and she languished in the sound. She'd missed this part of him.

Molly disconnected, took a long swig of her tea and walked the glass to the kitchen. Though she had certainly dressed casual after school, her outfit didn't do a thing for her. She marched into her bedroom and peered into the closet. After pulling out endless possibilities, she finally settled on beige-and-black capris with a beige knit top. She liked the scoop neckline, and the hue complemented her hair color.

She applied makeup, fussing over every line, combed her hair with a side part and grasped the scrunchie for her ponytail. "Ponytails are for kids." She winced, hearing her voice. Lately she'd begun talking to herself. She let her hair hang against her shoulders, appraising it from all directions. Good. She dropped the comb and strode through the doorway, looking for her sandals.

The drive to Brent's was etched in her mind. She admired the lovely homes as she meandered through the curved streets with unexpected cul-de-sacs that his neighborhood called circles. Each house had wonderful landscaping with flowers tucked beneath well-trimmed shrubs and broad lawns where dogs could run and play. She'd never been inside, and today she looked forward to seeing Brent's home.

She parked outside and headed up the walk, surprised when the door opened before she reached the brick porch. A wonderful aroma drifted to her as his playful tone caused her to wonder. "Something smells good."

"Let's hope dinner *tastes* good." He gave her a playful grin, his eyes scanning her hair. "Your hair looks great."

"Thanks." She wasn't sure whether to feel at ease or anxious.

Brent pushed back the screen door and

she stepped inside, wanting to talk about his home but instead blurting the question that had worried her. "Do you think my revisions are going to help my case?"

He rested his hands on her shoulders. "I'm not sure what they're going to do, but this has nothing to do with that. I figured you wouldn't come if I just invited you here."

She studied the tender look in his eyes.

"I'm sorry for the past week or so." He rubbed his temple. "When I don't know how to handle something, I tend to walk away until I can get myself together."

The warmth of his hands didn't compensate for the chill of failure in her heart. "Are you saying you can't handle me?"

A tender look spread over his face. "No. I can't handle myself."

"Huh?"

He released her shoulders and drew her elbow into the crook of his arm. "Let's go to the kitchen before I burn our dinner."

Though wondering about what he thought of her new report, she couldn't ignore the rich scent that drew her to follow. Coming through the doorway, she noticed a pot simmering on the stove. Brent released her arm, lifted the lid and dragged a wooden spoon through the meaty mixture.

"Is that chicken?" She headed his way, her stomach reminding her she'd skipped lunch.

"Paprikash."

"Chicken paprikash? I'm impressed." She moved beside him, letting her concerns be covered by the thought of the succulent dish he'd prepared. "You did this from scratch?"

"It's my mother's recipe. Her grandmother was Hungarian." He lifted a file card and flashed it in front of her.

His mother. Brent rarely spoke of her. Molly took the recipe and read the ingredients, amazed that he really cooked.

"Try it," he said, dipping a teaspoon into the sauce and bringing it to her lips.

"That's delicious." She scanned the yellowed card again. "Do you make the spaetzel noodles, too?"

He arched a brow. "Never tried. I think that's beyond me."

"How about if I give it a try?" Standing beside him in the kitchen felt perfect. Two people working together, talking about everyday things, being good friends. Her pulse skipped up her arm. "I've seen my mom make them."

"Sure, if you know how and if I have the ingredients."

Molly told him what she needed, and while he gathered the items, she filled a large pot with water and placed it on the burner. She loved the feeling of hominess she felt in the kitchen and sensed in Brent's demeanor.

While he watched, she mixed flour, eggs, a dash of salt and a sprinkle of parsley and water and then mixed the dough, searching for the right consistency. She dribbled in more water. "Did Rocket go to your dad's house with Randy?"

"He's in the backyard. I didn't want to wear Dad out." He left her side and wandered to the window, a different look on his face. "Speaking of my dad," he said, turning back and lowering his gaze and watching her pile the dough onto a cutting board, "we had a talk."

"A good one?"

He nodded. "I think so. Time will tell, but it makes a difference to me."

"I'm glad, Brent." She opened a drawer and pulled out a butter knife. "Would you like to talk about it?"

"Not really."

His rebuff disappointed her. "I'm happy you made some progress."

"Me, too." He stepped away and stirred the paprikash again. "How long will those take?"

"Not too long." The water simmered while

she used a small cutting board to scrape off small dollops of dough, letting them drop into the water.

"Don't rush. The paprikash still needs time." He gave it another stir.

As the spaetzel rose to the surface, she ladled them into a strainer Brent had found for her, and when all the dough had been cooked, she turned off the burner. "Before we eat, I'll just brown these in a fry pan with butter and some breadcrumbs, if you have them."

He pulled out a fry pan and placed it on the burner. She poured half of the spaetzel into the skillet with a glob of butter and a few crumbs. "Let the rest cool and you can freeze them for another time."

He stepped closer and brushed a wisp of hair from her cheek. "How about sitting for a while. I can keep an eye on this chicken. It shouldn't be too long."

His touch waffled through her chest.

When Brent strode away, she followed him into the great room. Though she'd been to the house before, she'd never been inside, and what she saw impressed her. Lacking the usual manly leather look, the room was graced with comfy furniture. No frills, but overstuffed easy chairs, a love seat and one recliner. The tables appeared to be walnut or maybe cherry with a warm tint that added friendliness to the room.

The carpet's earth tones drew in the outdoors, and through the window, the landscape spread before her with Rocket lying on the grass watching birds dip into the birdbath. "Your home is lovely."

"Thanks." He motioned for her to sit.

She chose a cozy easy chair. "You surprised me with that recipe of your mother's. Tell me about her."

"She died a couple years ago. Not much to tell. She supported my dad in the business and was involved in some church activities."

She'd never heard Brent mention religion. "Do you go to the same church?"

His smile faded. "God and I had a falling out a number of years ago."

"I'd say you had the falling out. God is faithful."

His look delved into her eyes. "That might be true."

"He hasn't given up on you. I hope you know that." As often as the weight of guilt pressed on her spirit, Molly knew God hadn't walked away. He'd forgiven her. She only needed to forgive herself.

Brent shifted in his chair. "Tell me about your parents."

She'd made him uneasy with her comment, and now she wondered where he and the Lord stood. Her emotions had already gotten out of control, but she knew nothing could move forward with Brent unless he loved the Lord as she did. "My parents are well and happy. They retired to Sedona and love it there."

"It's a beautiful place." He rose. "I need to stir the chicken."

Rocket's woof outside the door caused her to rise. "Can I let the dog in? He's barking."

"Go ahead."

She opened the door, and Rocket bolted in, leaping around her as she decided to let that be his next lesson. "Sit."

He did one small skip before he stopped and sat.

Pleased, Molly wished she had a nugget. She headed into the kitchen and snatched one from his doggie dish. When she turned, Rocket had followed. "Sit."

He did.

"Good boy." Molly slipped him the food and then settled beside Brent. "Randy's doing a good job with Rocket."

He smiled. "He's trying." He placed the spoon on a plate. "Just a few more minutes. I added the sour cream, and it needs to thicken." He motioned her back to the living room.

She suspected the food was ready, since he'd turned off the burner, but she hoped maybe he'd decided to tell her about his father, so she followed him back and sat in the easy chair, waiting.

"I wanted to say a couple of things before we eat."

"About the propos—"

"About us."

Her chest squeezed. "Us? What about us?"

"This has been on my mind all day, and I need to get it off my chest."

The thunder of her heart pounded in her ears.

"I'm like the sea, Molly. My emotions rise and fall with the tide. My aloofness or whatever you want to call it comes from my own confusion. I've given myself a talking-to, and I owe you an apology for dragging you through the mire of my uncertainty."

She studied his face. "I have no idea what you're telling me."

"I'm not good with words. Put me behind my desk or at a business meeting, and I'm in control. Put me in front of you and I'm a mess."

A mess? Her head spun. She still didn't understand.

Tension grew on his face. "I've confused you."

"You're observant."

A faint grin stole to his lips. "I like you, Molly. A lot."

Not what she expected. Her stomach joined her emotional fray, and she opened her mouth with the truth. "I like you, too."

"Liking you is my problem. I don't date. I just don't have anything to give a woman."

"You don't what?" She widened her eyes to emphasize her disbelief. "Brent, I love your patience. You listened to my crazy idea and accepted it. You became a supporter, even though I know you first thought I was nuts. You're kind. You've taken Randy into your life, and you're amazing. You adopted Rocket, even though you aren't partial to dogs for some reason. I know that's part of your past. Something you don't want to share."

"You see all that in me?"

"It's not on the outside. It's what's in —"

"The heart."

The two words rolled through her. "Yes. The heart. You can try to hide behind your defenses, but I look deeper. I have teacher's eyes. We see everything."

"I guess." He fell back against the recliner. "So what do we do now?"

His question knocked the wind out of her. She didn't know what she wanted, but she knew one thing. "Let's take time to explore our friendship. Will you agree that we've become friends?"

"Friends and cohorts in your project." He rose and extended his hand.

She stood and accepted his broad palm, her eyes exploring Brent's — deeper blue than a summer evening. Instead of releasing her hand, he drew her closer and wrapped one arm around her while his free hand stroked her hair.

She leaned against his strong chest and could have stayed there forever, but a loud clang from the kitchen dragged them apart.

Brent bolted toward the noise as Rocket shot through the breakfast doorway. "Rocket. What have you done?"

Molly and Rocket stared at each other while Brent stood in the kitchen doorway with a startled look on his face. She knew the dog had done something, but nothing would be worse than Rocket's timing.

"You rotten dog." Brent's voice sailed from the kitchen.

Molly hurried through the doorway to see the frypan on the floor with only a few pieces of spaetzel still inside.

"He ate it."

She eyed the few noodles left and tried not to laugh. "I don't suppose this can fall under the five-seconds rule."

"Five seconds?"

"When something falls, if you can pick it up in five seconds it's still edible." The look on his face and the situation released her laughter. "You know the ones I told you to freeze?"

He nodded.

"Don't."

CHAPTER NINE

Brent sat with his hands folded, waiting for a comment from the board. They had flipped open the proposal with the new information. Some sat with their hands folded while others seemed to be searching for something specific within the document.

"I believe Miss Manning has shown us that she is ready to make her own financial commitment. She has indicated she has fifty thousand dollars in ready cash, and an outside party willing to make monthly contributions equaling five thousand dollars each year. A veterinarian has donated time each month, and a pet store will provide a monthly supply of dog food for the first year."

Brent focused on each person, trying to read their expressions. "I believe Mo— Miss Manning has shown her commitment to the project, and we can cooperate by allowing her to use the building until —"

"If she has ready cash and we were interested in renting this building, why should we give it to her rent free?"

Brent straightened his shoulders, startled that the board member had missed the point. "The funds she has available are needed for start-up costs, revisions to the building, furnishings."

"Excuse me, but wasn't that something we discussed last week? What if she renovates the building so that we can't sell it as a —"

Brent's dander rose. "Jack, yes we did discuss this. I answered your concern at our last meeting. We're not talking major revisions. She will partition various areas to separate the waiting room and office areas from the kennel. These partitions can be easily removed."

"At whose expense, Brent?"

He eyed Jack, trying to decide why he was fighting the proposal. "The building is empty and has been for over two years. It's been sitting there. It's not selling and won't be with the economy as it is. Would it not be a gesture of benevolence to allow this young woman to create a shelter for dogs?" Brent grasped for Molly's statistics, hanging somewhere in his memory. "Did you know that between five and eight million animals are euthanized each year in the United States because they haven't had the opportunity to become adoptable by people who would give them a good home?"

"Look, Brent," Casey Dallis said, "you seem to love animals."

Brent stiffened. No, he didn't like . . . The lie failed him.

"But we're talking economics here, and it seems we could use this property for something more useful than a dog shelter. I just think —"

"Interesting."

Brent's father's voice cut through the icy air, and Brent went cold. "Dad, what are you doing here?" His long struggle to be the company director fell to its death on the boardroom floor.

His father sauntered in, pulled out a chair and sat. He eyed the board without looking at Brent. "Casey, what do you think we should do with the property?"

"Sell it and —"

"Then you haven't been listening." Morris leaned forward and stared the man in the eyes. "The property has been up for sale too long — years. The price has been cut to bare bones. No one is buying right now. Places are closing, not opening. Yes, one day it will change, and then we'll have this

194

building to sell at the price it's worth, but now, we'd have to give it away."

Jack's voice cut through the tension. "Isn't that what Brent is suggesting?"

"That's not what I'm suggesting, Jack. We're allowing this building to be used for a charitable cause and benefiting from an additional tax write-off."

Jack fell back against his chair and didn't respond.

Morris gestured to Brent to proceed, but Brent felt stifled by his father's interference. They'd just made steps to improve their relationship, and today he watched it slide into the sewer. He opened his mouth to tell his father to take over the meeting but stopped himself. Antagonism would get him nowhere, and his father had come in support. Molly would be devastated if her project fell apart at this point.

Brent drew up his shoulders. "Any more discussion or comments?"

Eyes lowered as his father stared them down.

"Our contract will be for two years with a renewal every two years, so we will have the opportunity to sell the building when the time is right. I'll personally see that the building is not altered in any way that might be a detriment to future use as a factory.

Miss Manning has already looked into registration of the facility, her licenses and the inspection requirements. She will carry insurance for the business as she stated in the proposal." He gazed around the room looking at heads pivoting from him to his father. "Are we ready for a motion?"

No new discussion rose. One of the quieter members mumbled the motion.

"Do I hear a second?"

To his surprise, Jack seconded the motion.

Brent kept his eyes steady. "Any more discussion?" Silence.

"All in favor of accepting this proposal as it has been amended, say aye."

Voices mumbled ayes around the table.

"Nays?"

None.

"The motion has passed." He shifted his gaze to his father. "Would you like to let Miss Manning know that her proposal has been accepted?"

His father's steady gaze lowered. "No. You're the director." He shifted his focus to the men at the table. "You've made a wise decision. Thank you. I would rather see this property used than be another example of our caving economy, and we're doing a service to this young woman and to the pets she cares about."

He rolled his chair back and rose. "Good day, gentlemen." He stepped toward the door and slipped silently out of the room while Brent sat trying to maintain his decorum.

The meeting dragged on for another hour, despite Brent's attempt to move it along. He realized Molly would be anxious to hear the news. When he saw the end coming, he pulled his cell phone from his pocket to see if he'd missed her call or perhaps a text message. None. His fingers tingled to call Molly and tell her the wonderful news.

After the men filed out and Brent sat in the room alone, he flipped out his cell and pressed in the first five numbers, then stopped. He'd miss the look on her face if he called. He stared at the buttons while his pulse raced and then slipped the phone back into his pocket. He didn't know how he could get through the day with out telling her. He took two steps and stopped. Directors could leave early any time they wanted to. Only he never did. Maybe today would be the first step to change his behavior.

Molly paced the floor until she grew impatient. She couldn't eat breakfast, and she'd tried lunch but struggled with every bite to swallow her sandwich. Anxious for Brent's call, she made a cup of tea and curled up on the sofa with a new novel. Summertime offered the luxury of reading her favorite authors' books she'd purchased and piled on the bookshelf.

The novel read well and presented an exciting story that should have captured her interest the moment she read the opening lines, but after three paragraphs she'd begun to read without meaning. She tossed the book on the lamp table and pulled out a magazine from the rack. She flipped through it, pulling out those irritating subscription cards lying between the pages and captured by the binding. She made a pile, and when she'd found them all, Molly walked into the kitchen and tore them into bits.

"Nothing like taking out my aggression on a magazine."

She shook her head, hearing her voice. Talking to herself had become a stress signal. Eyeing the bowl of fresh fruit on the counter, Molly dropped the last bit of paper into the wastebasket, admitting she'd felt light-headed all morning. Maybe she needed potassium. She grasped a banana from the bowl, dropped the peel in the trash and nibbled on it as she returned to the sofa, checking her watch for the umpteenth time.

It was after three. Her chest was weighted with worry. She'd thought Brent's board met in the morning.

Her chest ached, and tears seeped along the rim of her lashes. Molly spun around and headed to the bathroom, trying to swallow the last of the banana. When she caught her reflection in the mirror, her face looked pinched, and a tension headache had begun in the cords of her neck.

Molly opened the medicine cabinet and spilled two aspirins into her palm. As she grabbed a glass, the doorbell rang. She turned on the tap, filled the glass with a few swallows of water and tossed down the pills. She charged down the hallway to the front door, mumbling she wasn't in the mood to take a survey, hear any news about new condo rules or buy cookies from anyone.

When Molly jerked open the door, she let out a gasp. "Brent." He didn't have to tell her. She saw the uncomfortable look on his face.

"I didn't mean to startle you."

She studied his serious expression. "You're here to break the bad news."

He peered at her through the screen. "Could I come in?"

The shock of seeing him on her porch dislodged her manners. Molly pushed open the door. "Please. I . . . I . . ." She got no further, fighting back her disappointment.

Brent slipped past her and stood in the doorway of her living room. "This is attractive, Molly."

She only nodded and pressed her fingers against her lips to contain an outburst of tears as she motioned toward the sofa.

He sat in the easy chair while she waited.

He pointed to a chair. "Aren't you going to sit?"

"You had the board meeting today. I've been waiting to hear what happened."

An indefinable look swept across his face, as he rose and walked toward her.

Tears brimmed her eyes. "I'm not going to faint when you give me the news. I'm ready."

He stood in front of her, his expression shifting to a surprise grin. "The proposal passed."

She studied his face. "The proposal —"

"Passed. The building is yours."

Her hand flew to her chest. "It's mine. Really?" Her heart felt as if it would explode.

"Yes." The grin grew to a smile.

Molly threw her arms around his neck and buried her face in his shoulders. Tears she so rarely shed poured from her eyes and soaked his shirt. Though she tried to contain her joy, the reality triggered another outburst.

Brent held her against him, rubbing her back in gentle circles. The longer she cried the closer he drew her.

Calming herself, Molly gazed at him, and her heart stopped. His eyes were closed, and emotion filled his face. Though she wanted to speak, words didn't come. Brent's eyelashes flickered, and he looked at her with a tenderness she'd never seen. "I'm happy for you, Molly. Really happy."

She raised herself on tiptoes and wrapped her arms around him more tightly. "I can't thank you enough. I'm overwhelmed. I'm —" She looked at him again, her gaze shifting from his glistening eyes to his well-shaped lips. They parted as if he might speak, but that notion vanished as she felt him draw her closer. Their mouths touched in a breathless rush of longing.

Her heart thundered, and as reality pummeled her senses, she pulled back, gasping for air.

Brent looked stunned. "Molly, I . . . I didn't mean to do that."

"Neither did I, but we did." The warmth of his lips clung to her mouth. "We're both . . ." What? "I'm ecstatic about the shelter, Brent. I can't account for my actions."

He shook his head. "I plead the fifth."

Molly burst into laughter, her confusion, anticipation, excitement masquerading as humor.

Brent's face relaxed. "I wanted to tell you in person. I know I scared you at first, so I hope you forgive me for that."

After that kiss, forgiveness wasn't an issue. She touched his cheek with her fingers, feeling his soft skin with a hint of growing stubble. "You've already been forgiven." The way he looked at her caused her to question if he'd read between the lines.

He cupped her face in his hands. "You're always optimistic."

"No. I just believe."

He lifted his hand and pressed his palm against her fingers. "Let's celebrate."

Celebrate. Her spirit lifted heavenward. "I'd like that."

She removed her fingers from his cheek, and Brent lowered his hands to her shoulders.

"I'll see if my dad will keep Randy for me."

"Don't do that. Let's do something with him, too."

"Are you sure?"

She wanted to brush the creases from his

face. "I'm certain. Let's go downtown."

"To Detroit?"

"To the Downtown River Days. They have some carnival rides, music, kids activities and fireworks tonight. I saw it in the paper this morning."

"You're just a barrelful of information, aren't you?" He tweaked her cheek.

"I thought you were going to say a barrelful of fun."

Brent drew her closer. "We'll find out how much fun you are tonight at the Downtown River Days. Randy will be thrilled."

"I hope so."

She pictured the lonely child that she longed to see laughing and playing like other boys his age. Tonight would definitely help.

Music carried to the streets from speakers as Brent linked his arm with Molly's. Randy strode along beside them, sometimes running ahead and turning around to make sure they were still there.

Tantalizing smells of barbecued pork and sausages drifted from the riverfront vendors, and Brent's stomach gave a tug almost as strong as his heart had lurched earlier in the day when he held Molly in his arms.

Brent couldn't believe that he'd kissed

her. The desire lashed over him like a giant wave and washed away his good sense, but he couldn't be sorry. Molly had kissed him back, and the experience rocked him. The day would have been perfect except for his father's interference. Once again he looked like Daddy's puppet to the board of directors. He'd begun to believe he'd made headway and had gained their respect as the new director. Five minutes of his father's appearance had undone months of work.

Molly's questioning look made him realize he'd tensed. He managed a smile and turned the topic to the Ferris wheel. "Want to ride?"

She looked up at the towering wheel and curled her nose. "I don't like to be scared."

Randy grasped her arm and laughed. "I'll hang on to you so you don't fall out."

She gave him a hug.

Brent noticed Randy's surprised yet pleased expression. It touched him to see the boy respond to Molly like he did.

"I really don't think three people will fit in those little benches."

Knowing she was wrong, Brent slipped his hand in hers. "Let's find out." He steered her to the ticket booth, ignoring her protestation.

Randy craned his neck upward as the

wheel rose and dropped in its wide circle. "I've never been on a Ferris wheel."

The comment turned Molly's playful grumbling to silence. When she looked at Brent, she felt weighted with emotion. "Then it's time you ride on one, Randy. Every kid should ride a Ferris wheel. Next we'll all go on the carousel."

"Carousel?" The word shot out of Brent's mouth. "Me, on a carousel?"

She arched a brow. "And me on a Ferris wheel?"

He slammed his mouth shut. Molly had a way with words.

The line moved forward, and the three of them squeezed into the seat, with Molly in the middle. Brent's arm pressed against the side of the seat, and he lifted it behind Molly. A young man slammed the safety bar closed, and it jerked upward. Randy let out a belly laugh and leaned over the edge.

Molly clasped his arm. "Careful. We don't want to lose you."

He looked down one more time and then grabbed the bar as they edged upward.

Observing the interaction, Brent recalled that Randy's mother had never paid as much attention to the boy as Molly has been. Self-centered seemed a good description for Joan. He couldn't deny she changed

Randy's diapers and fed him, but he never recalled a motherly manner that women seemed to have naturally. Randall had been a better father. Brent recalled him sitting on the floor with Randy, putting together puzzles or playing with miniature cars.

The memory rattled him, especially thinking of Randall in a positive light. Brent would rarely admit to his brother doing anything but taunting him and enjoying it. Yet he'd been a good father. How easy it was to condemn someone when the judgment was biased. And Brent knew he had an attitude about his brother.

Molly let out a yell, and Randy's laughter brought him back from his memories. The wheel had been filled with new passengers, and they'd begun sweeping through the sky, dipping down toward the ground and then circling up again. He slid his arm down around Molly's shoulders, and she glanced his way, her smile brighter than the colorful carnival lights.

"Are you scared?" Randy called out as the wheel took another dip, his giggles nearly covering his words.

"Never," Molly said, grinning back at Brent.

When the ride ended, Molly led them to the carousel, and though he felt foolish,

Brent climbed aboard and mounted a horse beside her. Randy charged onto a chubby pig, looking over his shoulder at them, his eyes filled with happiness as the carousel's music tooted and the ride revolved.

Such simple pleasures. Randy's glee filled Brent's heart. "He's having a blast."

"You're not." Her look probed for a response.

He drew back. "Why do you say that?"

"Something's on your mind. I noticed it earlier."

Brent wasn't surprised. The woman was uncanny. She read his mind. He gave her a quick nod, wishing he could hide his feelings from her yet relieved that she'd brought it out in the open. She'd asked so often for him to tell her what bothered him. She didn't understand that men didn't want to talk about feelings. Still today, he wanted to tell her about the setback.

"Later." He flashed a look at Randy. She nodded as if she understood.

The ride didn't last as long as his mortification when he climbed off and saw one of his employees. The man gave him a nod, his face emblazoned with a grin, and Brent gave the man a wave and scurried away, feeling like a kid trying to hide a misdeed from his parents.

Molly followed the man with her eyes. "You know him?"

"He works for me."

Molly let out a soft chuckle. "Now he knows you're a good sport."

Randy edged between them. "Where's the kids' stuff? You said they had special things for kids to do."

Molly put her arm around his shoulders and gave him a squeeze. "Let's find it. Look for an Arrghs and Crafts sign."

Brent did a double take. "Did I hear you right? Arrghs and crafts?"

"It's called Pirates Cove. They'll turn Randy into a swashbuckling pirate."

Randy's eyes lit up. "*Pirates of the Caribbean.* I could be Jack Sparrow."

Molly grinned and manufactured a laughable pirate's voice. "Then let's go, matey."

Brent followed Molly's direction along the riverwalk to the Rivard Plaza. Brent paid for Randy's pirate hat and someone gave him an eye patch. They checked out the activities, and while Randy had a pirate tattoo painted on his arm, Brent and Molly stood back and watched.

Music resounded from loudspeakers, and Brent pulled Molly against him, her back leaning on his chest. He rocked to the rhythm of the music while one emotion crashed against another — emotions so new and wonderful he felt overwhelmed. Though he cautioned himself to be careful, the relationship had picked up momentum like a roller coaster heading downhill. Caught in a whirlwind of feelings, he lost grasp of his center. All he could do was hang on.

The last thing he wanted was to hurt Molly. If he tried to explain his doubts about a relationship, most people would think he was crazy. He'd be sent away in a white coat, his arms tied behind his back. Pleasure rose in his chest as he felt his arms pressed against Molly's smooth skin. He leaned around to kiss her cheek, amazed at the softness.

Molly glanced over her shoulder with a look that melted his heart. "You're a good man, Mr. Runyan."

"You're amazing, Miss Manning." He tightened his embrace.

"I'm hungry," Randy called, bounding toward them, flashing his artificial tattoo.

Hating to let Molly go, Brent yielded to Randy's hunger, and they headed toward the refreshment area, his own unresolvable hunger raging in his heart.

CHAPTER TEN

The fireworks still glowed in Molly's mind as they headed home. The long afternoon and evening had tired Randy. He'd curled up on the small backseat and had fallen asleep before they wound their way out of the parking structure. His pirate hat had toppled to the floor, and his tattooed arm lay beneath his head for a pillow.

Molly released a long sigh. "This was a great day. Thanks."

Brent shifted his hand from the steering wheel to hers. "Randy had such a good time. Today I realized how much he's missed. Not just his parents, but things kids do. He's been stuck in a world with old people — me included — who forget what it was like to be a child."

"That's why there are circuses and amusement parks. So we don't forget." She rolled her hand palm up beneath his and wove her fingers through his. "They allow adults to be children again, too, with no guilt."

Brent remained silent. He lifted his hand and grasped the steering wheel. "No guilt? I wish."

Holding back the seat belt, Molly shifted onto her hip. "You're not to blame for Randy's situation. Things happen. You and your parents did the best you knew how to do."

"I do feel to blame."

"That doesn't make sense."

"I know how I feel, Molly. For one thing, I shouldn't have been so selfish. I let Randy stay with my parents when I should have taken him in."

"You're younger, yes, but you have a job. Your mom was home, and they had a house-keeper. Someone was there for Randy all day."

"My mom had her commitments, too. You can't leave a housekeeper to raise a child who lost both parents."

"Where is Randy's mother?"

Brent shrugged. "We've never heard from her. She just walked away. Said she couldn't be a good mother. Joan had emotional problems from the start, I guess."

Molly's heart felt torn from her chest. "It's awful." She glanced into the backseat. Randy's even breathing assured her he was

211

asleep. When she turned back, she rested her hand on Brent's leg and gave it a pat. Brent's life had been filled with difficult times despite his family's wealth. Once again God's Word proved true. Don't store up treasures on earth that can rust or be stolen, but lay up treasures in heaven. *For where your treasure is, there your heart will be also.* Brent had a good heart. He'd just been misguided along the way. Her prayer rose that the Lord open Brent's eyes to the true treasures in his life.

She squeezed Brent's leg and withdrew her hand. "What upset you today? You said you'd tell me later."

Brent's body sagged with her question. She'd asked at the wrong time. Randy was in the car and he couldn't focus on driving with all that in his mind.

"I promise to tell you. Just not now." He became thoughtful for a moment.

Molly glanced over the seat again. "He's quite a boy. I see changes, and they're for the good."

"And I give you the credit."

"Me?" She shook her head, astounded at his conclusion. "Why?"

"You've encouraged me to get the dog, to bring Randy here today, to help him find himself."

"You helped him find love, Brent. It's love that's so important. *'And now these three remain: faith, hope and love. But the greatest of these is love.'*"

"1 Corinthians 13:13."

Her spirit sang. "Yes. You know the verse."

"I know it."

She waited.

"But I don't live it, Molly. That's the crux of my problem."

She slipped back against the seat cushion, perplexed. Her mind swung from situation to situation, trying to make sense of his conclusion.

A deep sigh rolled from his chest. "I don't know how to love."

The comment knocked the wind from her. She gathered her emotions and constrained them. "Brent, don't ever say that again. Love is part of our being. It's from the Lord. You can reject love, but it's innate. Even the most evil person in the world has love for his mother or child. Maybe his dog. You don't know what love is. Maybe that's your problem."

He glanced her way, then back to the road. "Tell me what love is, Molly."

"It's something in your heart, in your being. When you feel sorrow or grief, it's because you love. When you feel concern or

213

longing, it's because you love. It's part of you. Sometimes love is tangled in traps we set for ourselves, and then we can't show it. We fear being rejected or being laughed at, but the love is still there."

Brent's breathing faltered. He drove in silence, his lips pressed together so tightly Molly wondered if he were stopping himself from speaking or controlling his emotions.

"I need to think about it." His voice came out like a ragged whisper.

Molly folded her hands in her lap. For once she knew when to remain silent. The lesson had taken so long to learn, but tonight she knew silence was truly golden.

Brent rinsed the dishes and tucked them into the dishwasher as Molly watched him. He'd missed her the past three days, and today her presence pumped his spirit more than one of those energy bars he kept hearing about on TV.

"I could have picked up Randy instead of your father driving here." Molly leaned against Brent's kitchen counter, a lopsided grin on her face as she watched his domestic skills, which he knew were lacking.

He wiped his hands on a dish towel. "Dad promised him dinner at a fast-food place tonight. Can you believe?"

"Not really." Her smile deepened. "Let's go outside with Rocket. I can show you what I have in mind for Randy today."

He tossed the dish towel on the rack. "Great. I can show you what I did, too."

She gave him a questioning look as he motioned her through the door off the breakfast room into the garage. He motioned her through the single door into the backyard. At their sound, Rocket pricked up his ears and bounded toward them, brushing his nose against Molly's pantleg. She knelt and rubbed the retriever behind the ears. "You're ready for your lesson, aren't you?"

While the dog nuzzled against her, Brent dipped inside the garage and brought out part of the surprise behind his back. Before he could show her, Molly had rounded the corner to the driveway and let out a screech. "A basketball hoop."

He darted past her, bouncing the ball on the concrete. He aimed at the hoop and swished one in. "Ready?"

Her hand flew to her chest. "Me?"

"You and Rocket. I'll beat you both."

She laughed, skipping past him to play defense while she tried not to trip over Rocket's eager maneuvers. Surprising him, Molly bounded behind his back and captured the ball. She dribbled it as she scooted backward, spun around, aimed, and the ball hit the backboard. Brent captured it in the blink of an eye. She charged forward to recover the ball, so focused she tripped over Rocket. As she barreled forward, Brent dropped the ball and caught her in the midst of her laughter. He wrapped his arms around her, his laugh joining hers while Rocket leaped at their feet, obviously ready to play some more.

When she'd caught her breath, Brent drew her closer. "You're lucky I was a Boy Scout."

"You were?"

He loved the look on her face. "No, but I always wanted to be." That was another want that died a quick death. No time for such foolishness, his father had said.

Molly's smile faded as she studied his face. "More memories."

He shrugged. "Silly things come to mind."

She touched his cheek. "You still haven't told me what —"

"Uncle Brent!"

Brent's arms slipped from Molly as guilt encompassed him. He turned toward Randy and winced, seeing his father advancing behind the boy. His appearance at the meeting still didn't sit well.

"I had chicken nuggets and fries." Randy

dropped his duffle bag on the edge of the driveway. "What were you and Molly doing?"

Brent bounced the ball, evading his father's curious look. "I was showing Molly your basketball hoop."

A questioning look settled on Randy's face as he studied Molly and then looked back at Brent.

Molly glowed from more than the sun. She'd stepped back, her hands in her pockets as if she wished she could hide in them. He couldn't help but grin, having the same feeling.

Trying to restrain the irritation he felt with his father, Brent managed a pleasant expression. "Thanks, Dad, for taking Randy out to dinner." He saw a knowing look in his father's eyes and glanced away as he wrapped his arm around Randy's shoulders. "You had fun with your grandpa."

Randy nodded.

"I heard all about the new hoop and about Molly."

Brent noticed his father eyeing Molly with a grin growing on his face.

Keeping his gaze on her, his father strode her way. "I'm glad you're here so I can thank you."

"Me?" She looked as bewildered as Brent

felt. "For what?"

Brent took a step closer, curious what his father had to say.

"Toss it here, Uncle Brent." Randy stood in front of the hoop, clapping his hands and beckoning for the basketball.

Brent tried to listen while Randy goaded him into a game, but he couldn't concentrate. Distracted by their conversation and Rocket's eternal playfulness, Brent fumbled the ball. Randy hooked it and made one of the best shots he'd ever made.

"Good for you," Brent said, giving him a high five. "That'll teach me not to pay attention." When he glanced toward Molly again, his father was shaking her hand.

"Want to give it a try, Dad?" He strode toward them, wishing he could have caught a shred of their conversation.

"You want to watch me keel over and die? I'm not ready for those pearly gates yet."

Brent noticed Molly's eyes widen. The expression made him curious.

"I'll let you get on with the obedience lesson." His father captured his faint grin by turning away. After two steps, he turned back. "You're doing a great job with them, Molly."

Them? A frown jumped to Brent's face. The lessons were Randy's.

"He's a good student, Mr. Runyan."

Brent shrank beneath his father's gaze before his dad refocused on Molly. "I'm sure, but I think you're an excellent teacher. You're working wonders." He strode toward Brent and squeezed his shoulder. "Speaking of wonders, Brent says the renovation is going well."

"Very well. You're welcome to stop by and see for yourself."

To Brent's surprise, his father gave her a wink. "I might just do that."

Molly headed their way. "My parents are coming in next week to help paint and get things organized. It'll look great when we get it done."

"I'll make it a point to stop by." He studied her a moment and then lifted his hand. "I'll be on my way and let you two get back to . . . the lessons."

Brent heard his father chuckle as he walked away, and he wanted to chase after him to deny everything, but his father had seen enough to suspect a romance.

Romance. The word sizzled through Brent. Friendship. He and Molly had a friendship. That's all he could handle, and it's all she wanted. She'd told him clearly enough.

When he looked back, Molly stood with

her hand on Randy's shoulder as they talked, and the boy's face shone like sunshine. He wondered if that's what his father had seen on his face.

"Do you want this door folding in or out?" The man balanced the door between his hands.

Molly looked at the opening. "In, and I want Dutch doors on the cubicles for the dogs. Did I tell you that?"

"It's on the blueprints?"

She shrugged. Naturally.

Her mind had taken a holiday, and at times, she wished she could take one, too. Between thoughts of the shelter, Brent, Randy, and now Morris's cryptic comments, she didn't know which way to turn. Standing inside her new office area with built-in shelves and storage, she could hardly believe the shelter would soon be a reality. She only had to stain the shelving, and the room was finished.

She'd been trying to work on a shoestring budget, as her mother called it. Her mom warned her over and over that she'd get what she paid for, but so far, she'd proved her mother wrong. In down times like these, the carpenters were happy to have work.

Next door to the office, they'd built a

clinic for the veterinary visits. She'd made a list of necessities for the room and hoped she could purchase used equipment or beg it from one of the vets who'd been so kind. Molly admitted that when it came to her shelter she wouldn't be too proud to use secondhand furnishings.

Down the hallway, hammers rang out, building the cubicles for the dogs. She'd dreamed of putting them in something other than a cage. They always seemed so heartless, and yet she knew cages were easier to keep clean. She hoped the inspectors would approve her idea.

Flipping open a notepad, Molly jotted down other items she'd remembered. Her shopping list was growing, but she suspected her mother would enjoy helping her with the project when her parents arrived next week. She pulled a pencil from behind her ear, and it flew from her fingers and rolled away. She crouched to retrieve it, holding her aching back.

"There you are."

Molly jumped up and spun around. "Brent. You scared me."

His gaze swept over her as a toying look spread over his face.

"I know I look a mess." She ran her fingers through her hair, feeling the wispy ends that had escaped the scrunchie.

"You look lovely."

She stuck out her tongue. "And you look like Pinocchio." She wiggled her nose.

He stepped closer. "How's it going?"

"Take a look." She motioned down the hall, followed by a sweeping motion to her office. "This room is done, except to stain the wood. Wander out and look at the rest."

"I will." He gave her an uneasy look. "Do you have a few minutes?"

"For what?" She gazed down at her dusty jeans and baggy top, thinking he'd come to paint.

"How about a coffee? There's a little restaurant down the street. We can walk."

A serious look rose in his eyes, and she nodded. "You take a look, and I'll get cleaned up." That was an exaggeration. She'd comb her hair.

While Brent toured the building, she sprinted into the restroom, pulled her ponytail from the elastic and combed her hair and then tied it up again. She flipped open her bag and drew out lipstick, dragging it across her lips. She looked pale after spending so much time inside. She'd missed her usual summer tan. Molly took a dab of color from the lipstick tube and blended it into her cheeks. Makeshift, but it worked.

Brent waited outside the office when she exited the restroom. They strolled outside together, and Molly was surprised at the warmth of the sun. Inside the concrete building the air remained cool. While the sun spread across her arms, her heart warmed beside Brent. He'd become a fixture in her life, their friendship growing.

Friendship. The word held little meaning to what she felt. But she needed time, and Brent had many wounds to heal before their relationship could flower into anything else — if it could at all.

"You're quiet." Brent's voice cut into her thoughts.

"I feel like a hermit hidden inside the building, but I want to get as much done as I can before my parents get here." She motioned to his attire. "You look like you came to help out."

"I did, but I haven't seen you for so long, and you mentioned on the phone you've made a lot of progress." He squeezed her hand. "I've missed you."

"Sorry about neglecting the lessons. When the shelter's finished, I can spend more time with Randy and Rocket."

He slipped his hand into hers as they strode into the next block. "I'm not talking about Randy and Rocket. I missed you, too.

223

I've wanted to talk to you about my dad and what happened."

She stopped and faced him. "What happened?"

"He's stubborn and domineering."

She took another step, not surprised at Brent's comment.

Brent grew quiet.

"Is that the problem?"

He faltered, shaking his head. "No, I'm the problem."

Her heart flew to her throat. "Brent, is something wrong?"

He shook his head. "Nothing like that." He grasped her hand and gave it a squeeze. "I'm still dealing with issues with my father. You know we had a good talk, and I thought things had finally fallen into place, but Dad has a hard time letting go."

"What did he do?"

"He marched into the board meeting the day of the proposal approval and swayed their decision."

Her breath hitched. "Swayed their decision? What does that mean?"

"I was fighting a losing battle, but I had more ammunition, and I was confident that I could convince them otherwise, but *Dad* came in and all but told them they had no choice."

"Really." She pictured those probing eyes of his that dug deep into people's confidence. He'd frightened her at first.

"You can thank my dad, not me, for the yes vote on your proposal."

She came to a stop. "Brent, if you hadn't agreed to go ahead with my proposal, it wouldn't have happened."

His head lowered, and he didn't respond.

"What?" Her mind spun with conjectures.

"My father insisted I pursue this with you. I can hardly take credit."

"You were against it?"

"No. I'd decided to go ahead with your idea, but before I could tell you, he barged in and gave me no choice."

Her disappointment eased while her curiosity grew. "Why?"

"I don't know. He said he liked your gutsiness." He gave a one-shoulder shrug. "He didn't say it that way, but that's what he meant. He likes decisive people who are like him." He stepped back and held up his hand. "I don't mean you're like my dad, but you have his determination."

"I've been told that before." She moved ahead toward the restaurant, Brent following, while her mind sorted through myriad questions.

In the middle of the next block, Brent

stopped in front of the restaurant and opened the door. The air-conditioned chill sent gooseflesh up Molly's arms. Hot coffee would taste good.

Brent motioned to a booth, and she slipped into the bench seat while he sat across from her. He folded his hands on the table. "I'm going to talk with Dad again. I don't like how I feel."

"About him?"

He nodded. "Frustrated. Resentful. Discouraged. I want a good relationship. It's been so long in coming. When I was a boy, my dad seemed like a stranger to me — not a stranger, exactly, but a giant who trudged through my life destroying everything I wanted."

"Something he said the last time I saw him gave me a surprise. Something about pearly gates. I didn't know your father was a Christian." She saw a flicker of distress in his face.

"Mom went to church, but Dad only went sometimes. Always on Easter and Christmas. They sent me to Sunday school, but I couldn't connect what I learned there with what I saw at home. The word *love* had little meaning for me. Yes, my parents were good. They provided me with an attractive home and wholesome food. They took me to the doctor and dentist. They saw to it that I did well in school, but I didn't sense the close relationship that other kids had with their parents. I couldn't comprehend the idea of Jesus being my personal friend. I just wanted friends I could see and play with."

Molly couldn't get a full breath, and a dizzy sensation made her feel helpless. "I'm sorry, Brent. They just didn't realize."

"They didn't live their faith the way I see you living it, and I know you are blessed for it."

Hearing Brent use the word *blessed* thrilled Molly. Today she knew for certain he had God in his heart. He'd just covered Him with his bitterness. Lord, open the door. "It's hard to think of your dad being like that. He seems as if he cares now. I realize you were irked at him for coming to the board meeting, but he cared enough to support the proposal."

"He has changed, I guess. The other day I joked about wanting to be a Boy Scout. I knew kids who were scouts. They earned medals for different activities, and it sounded like fun. My dad said it was a waste of time. I should use my time to study so I could make something of myself. It's those things I have a hard time letting go of when I see what a mess I am today. Back then, he forgot that kids also needed friends and —"

"Time to be kids."

"Right. Time to be kids."

The waitress arrived with menus. Molly ordered coffee, but Brent added two pieces of strawberry rhubarb pie to his drink order. The woman placed two napkins along with forks and spoons on the table and then left.

"That's why I'm so happy you took Randy." Molly slid the napkin from the table and spread it on her lap.

"I am, too. The kid is thrilled with the littlest thing. He's not the same boy anymore. I'm seeing him take responsibility with the dog. He's eager to help me with the lawn mowing. I don't think he'd ever mowed a lawn before, and he's capable."

"I knew that when he was in my special-ed class. He needed attention. That's what I saw." She opened her mouth to add "and love," but she knew Brent understood that now.

"You've done a lot for him with the basketball hoop and the dog."

"And I'm buying him a bike for his birthday. It's coming up in two weeks. He's never had a bike, except for a tricycle when he was a little kid."

A smile grew on her face, picturing Randy's excitement with a bike. "He'll love that."

"I think so."

The waitress reappeared with their drinks and pie and set the bill on the edge of the table before she walked away.

Molly lifted her cup. "I'll have to think of something special for Randy's birthday, too."

"You're something special, Molly. He's crazy about you. He talks about you all the time."

"Really?" She wasn't sure she liked that. What would happen if she vanished from his life? The child had lost so many people. Molly didn't want to be another one who walked away, leaving him feeling abandoned once again.

"You know how he feels."

But she didn't. Not really. She looked up and gazed at Brent. She wasn't sure how he felt, either. The whole relationship thing rattled her.

"I understand Dad a little better now, but I still need to talk with him about his manipulation at the meeting."

"Don't be too rough on him, Brent. It's hard to change sometimes. He'd been the president of the company for years."

"He still is, but I'm the director. If he'd

lived, it would have been Randall."

"Why? Because he was older?"

"No, because he was Dad's main focus."

She squirmed in the seat, not wanting to hear him talk like that. "You mean his favorite? Why would you say that?"

"It's too long and involved. One day, I'll tell you the whole story, but in a nutshell, Randall had charisma. He could manipulate his way into the Oval Office if he wanted to."

"I doubt that." She grinned, hoping to lighten the depressing conversation.

"You know what I mean."

"You may have felt that way, but I don't see it. Your father's proud of you. It's obvious."

He looked into Molly's eyes. "He said that to me the other day. I never thought I'd hear it, but I did."

"Brent, things happen in God's time, not ours. There are things we all want to hear in our lives and fear we never will." Her pulse skipped. Somehow mixed in her swinging pendulum of emotions, the word *love* came to mind. Would she ever hear the romantic words, "I love you?"

CHAPTER ELEVEN

Brent relaxed against the cushion in his father's study, digesting the talk he'd had with his dad. He didn't want to be wrong, but as he thought about what Molly said and heard his father's reasoning, it made sense. His biased judgment had not allowed him to see his father as his ally. He picked a piece of lint from his dark pants and headed in a new direction. "Since we're being open and honest, I'm curious about something. Molly asked about your faith, and I suppose I have the same question. She seemed surprised that you're a Christian. Why didn't you attend church regularly?"

His father gave him a thoughtful look. "I'm sorry about that, Brent. I don't suppose I was a good example. I always knew God existed, but I had a difficult time with the whys of faith. Why did bad people succeed? Why did hardworking people have to struggle to stay that way? Why did He allow

231

me to be a parent and feel so inadequate?"

Brent felt he'd been struck. "You felt like that?"

"Certainly." He lowered his head. "I don't suppose I let you know that . . . or your mother, either, for that matter. I tried to leave you boys in her hands, figuring she had a more maternal bent then I did."

"She wasn't around much, either." Brent rose, his arms flailing without direction. "Did you realize the housekeeper did more with us than you and even Mom did?"

His father flinched, the color growing on his cheeks as if he'd been slapped.

Brent dropped his arms to his sides. "I don't mean to sound so harsh, and I should correct that. You did take time to teach Randall how to hunt."

"You never wanted to. You liked books, and I counted on you one day to take over the business."

"You wanted me?" He froze in place.

"I wanted that more than realizing you needed time to be a kid, I suppose."

"I always thought —"

"Randy was different than you. He wanted a good time. He wanted to joke around, and he had a cocky attitude that I should have knocked out of him long before he grew up and got himself in that marriage. Your mother and I knew it was wrong. Joan wasn't a woman to be a mother, but she'd gotten pregnant and —"

Brent felt the blood drain from his face. "Before they married?"

His dad looked away and nodded. "It was the worst day of our lives up to then."

"I never knew that."

"But you were our pride and joy, Brent. I worked you hard. I expected things of you, and I did it so wrong."

This wasn't time to ease his father's grief. It was time for honesty. He tucked his hands into his pockets and forced himself to look into his father's eyes. "Yes, you did."

"I don't expect your forgiveness, Brent. I only hope that I can make up for it some way in the years I have left."

"Forgiveness isn't an issue. You're my father. You obviously did your best. You said that, and I understand. It's as much my fault. I didn't say anything. I kept it bottled up inside of me."

"I wish you hadn't. Still, you've come through it more than you seem to realize. You're making good decisions at the company. I only came, as I said, to support you."

Their talk had opened so many doors. Brent thought about his resentment over the years, his misconstrued idea of his father's plans for the company and attitudes about Randall. He flinched beneath the weight of his mistakes. Even his attitude toward God had been misguided.

"And Molly."

Her name catapulted his pulse.

"I can see right through her."

Brent's hands jerked from his pockets and dropped to his side. "See right through her? You mean she has an ulterior motive?"

His father's serious expression broke into a smile. "Not at all. I think she charged into our lives and made us both different people. I love her compassion and enthusiasm — her drive and her openness. I was referring to her transparent feelings. I can see her love for animals and her purpose. She's crazy about Randy and Rocket, and I can see how she feels about you."

His heart stopped. He waited, but his father didn't expand. "She thinks I'm a mess."

"Maybe, but she sees your heart, too, and she loves what she sees."

He sounded like Molly. She'd talked about looking inside a person and seeing their heart, but his dad was very wrong. "No. Molly made it very clear that she was only open to a friendship."

His father laughed. "Have you ever known

234

a woman who didn't change her mind?"

He searched his father's face. He wasn't joking. Brent released a ragged breath and sank into the chair. Could his father be correct? Molly? His mind whirled.

"So nice to meet you." Molly's mother shook Brent's hand. "And you must be Brent's father. I can see it through the eyes. You both have a sparkle." She grasped Morris's hand and gave it a firm shake as the retriever stood beside her wagging his tail. "And you're Rocket." She reached down and gave the dog a pet while his tail whacked against Brent's pant leg. "Where's the young man that belongs to this sweet dog? Molly's told me all about him."

Brent smiled. "He's inside. He wanted to mix some lemonade for everyone. May be I should go in and make sure —"

"Let me go," Molly said, "and I'll see what's keeping Dad. He only had the cooler to carry back here."

She darted past the garage, looked in the driveway and spotted her dad bent over the cooler as he placed items back inside.

"What happened?" Molly hurried to his side.

He looked up and grinned. "I was careless. It slipped out of one hand and I hadn't locked the top." He lifted his hands in the air with a helpless gesture. "Just careless. Have I missed the celebration?"

"It doesn't start without you." She kissed him on the cheek as she gathered up two more bottles of soft drink. "Randy's making lemonade, so make sure you have some of that."

He gave her a wink as he closed the lid. "Definitely." He stood and hoisted the cooler.

"Want some help?" Molly reached for a handle.

He gave her a playful frown. "And look like a wimp?"

"Never." She gestured toward the house. "Then I'm on a mission. I'm to check on Randy." She darted off, opened the front door and veered through the dining room into the kitchen. She stopped short. "How's it going?" She assumed Randy was making concentrated lemonade, but he had a pile of lemons and a juicer in front of him.

"I'm almost done."

She strode to his side. "You're doing it the hard way."

He pushed the lemon half onto the juicer. "I know. Uncle Brent said we should use the frozen stuff, but I wanted to make real lemonade."

236

She put her arm around his shoulders. "Can I get the sugar for you?"

"Okay. It's in the cabinet over there." He motioned with his head.

Molly picked the wrong one but found it on her second try. Seeing Randy more outgoing and confident touched her. She couldn't imagine the loneliness he had felt so much of his life. Too much like Brent. They'd been raised the same under different circumstances, but God had blessed them both with His healing hand. She prayed every night that the Lord make things right for both of them.

"How much sugar do you need?"

He looked at the recipe on the counter. "For ten lemons it says four scoops."

Molly pursed her lips. "Scoops? What size?"

Randy shrugged. "Let's use a smaller one and taste it after each scoop."

"Brilliant. Why didn't I think of that?"

" 'Cuz I did."

They both laughed, and using a four-ounce scoop, they got it just right. Randy stirred the mixture with a long spoon and then carried the pitcher while Molly grabbed the paper cups and headed outside.

By the time they reached the others, her father had been introduced, and he and

Morris were talking together near the barbecue. She set the cups on the picnic table and let Randy take the honors of filling the glasses.

Brent introduced Randy to Molly's mother, and after he'd hustled off to fill the glasses, Brent and her mother talked about his house and business. Molly listened, noticing that Brent seemed comfortable with her. Her mother had even accepted his Fourth of July barbecue with a smile.

Excusing himself, Brent strode away to bring out the meat for the grill, and when he was out of earshot, Molly moved beside her mother. "What do you think of Randy?"

"He's a sweet boy." Her gaze probed Molly's. "And what do you think about Brent?"

Molly drew back, noticing the look in her mother's eyes. "He's a great guy. He's been so supportive of the dog shelter." She gestured toward Morris, hoping to distract her mother. "Brent's father has been great, too. He went to the board of directors in support of my proposal."

"I think you're more than that to Brent."

"Mom!" Too late to monitor her exclamation, she noticed the two men had stopped talking and stared at her. She checked her volume. "Please. We're friends."

Her mother arched an eyebrow.

"Really. Brent has issues, and I . . . I do too."

"Issues? You?"

Molly's head pivoted toward her dad and Morris, hoping they hadn't heard her comment, but before she could respond, Randy appeared with the lemonade. Bad timing. Now her mother would bug her about her stupid slip. Using any word other than *issues* would have been better. She didn't want to bring up the past.

Molly took a glass from Randy and handed it to her mother and then took one for herself. The door opened, and Brent came through the garage carrying a tray of meat. As he neared, he tilted his head toward he house. "If you want to toss a salad, you can, and we need the corn husked."

"Sure thing." Molly grasped the reprieve and turned toward the house.

Her mother fell into step. "I'd be happy to husk corn."

Definitely, and Molly would be cornered. She lifted her shoulders, accepting that she might as well face the grilling now instead of later.

Her mother followed her into the kitchen and headed for the corn. She tore open the bag and pulled out the ears.

Molly filled a large pot with water and popped it on the burner, enjoying the respite. Maybe her mother had forgotten her slip of the tongue, and she could avoid the interrogation about her relationship with Brent. Molly dug into the refrigerator and pulled out the greens and vegetables for the salad. They worked in silence for a few moments until her mother asked for a knife to cut off the cob ends.

Molly motioned to a drawer, and after her mother pulled out a wide-blade knife, she leaned against the counter. "What issues?"

Molly jerked to attention.

"You said you had issues. I'm your mother. You can talk with me."

"It's nothing, Mom. Yes, I do think a lot of Brent, but —" Molly eyed the knife clutched in her mother's hand. "It's just that . . . I don't want to make any mistakes."

"A mistake? I can see he cares about you. It's obvious."

Obvious? Molly tried to concentrate on the vegetables while dealing with the fact that she couldn't hide her feelings from anyone.

"So what's the problem?"

Her mother's probing made her head swim. She felt like a teen again, having to face her parents when she'd messed up.

Molly pulled air into her lungs, hoping to sway the conversation. "He's not a strong believer. I worry about that."

"It's good you're aware of that, but Christians sometimes fall by the wayside and only need loving hands to ease them back. You can provide an example, and he'll come around. If the Holy Spirit finds a crack in his armor, He gets inside. God's love outshines the darkness. Brent will find the light."

"I know, Mom, but —"

"Then what else is an issue?" Her mother tilted her head with a mother's penetrating gaze. "That must not be all of it."

Her mother had a way of delving into her head and dragging out things that Molly had no intention of sharing. "He doesn't know, Mom."

"Is that important now, Molly? The Lord wiped your sins away."

"If anything's to come of our . . . relationship, I want him to know."

Her mother nodded. "You're right. I don't keep things from your father, either. Then tell him. But it won't make a difference, Molly, not if he loves you."

The words flattened Molly. Love did shine through the darkness. She'd said it herself.

Her mother wrapped an arm around her

shoulder. "You're a good woman. You went astray but you came back, and God's cleaned your slate." She tilted Molly's head so their eyes met. "You've worked so hard to prove yourself. You don't settle for second best. You want to give God the best."

"I do that, Mom. I want to be perfect like you and Dad. You do everything right. You don't have problems. You make the right decisions. You never argue."

Her mother's hand shot up and she drew back. "Hold it." She placed her palm on Molly's shoulder and shook her head. "Molly, you're living under a delusion."

"No, I'm not. I saw it with my own eyes. I lived with you most of my life."

"I know you did, but you didn't hear and see everything."

Molly stood still. "But —"

"If you think your dad and I didn't have arguments and get angry, you're totally mistaken. We didn't argue in front of you kids. We tried to air our problems privately and resolve them without getting all of you worried."

"You and Dad had serious problems?"

"They were at the time. Marriage isn't easy, Molly. It takes work. People have to give and take. They have to think of each other instead of themselves, but they can't lose their own identity, either. Marriage is a partnership. It's two people agreeing to disagree at times but loving every minute of it."

"What about Nolan and Amy? Their marriage didn't last."

"Your sister and brother didn't work at it. They gave up too early. A marriage can work if both parties want it and if they work together."

"I know it takes two."

Her mother slipped her arms around Molly's shoulder. "You and Brent undertook the task of making the shelter a reality, and his father even joined in, which shows he's a good man. You've both made a young boy happy, a boy who had some awful things happen to him at an early age, and yet he's such a nice kid."

Molly's throat tightened, and she drained of energy. "What will happen to Randy if Brent and I aren't meant to be? What if —"

"Don't worry about what-ifs." Her mother opened her arms, the knife slicing the air. Molly ducked. Her mom gaped at the blade, and they both laughed as she dropped it on the counter as Molly's concerns eased in the slapstick moment.

Without the knife, her mom embraced her, holding her close. "You need the Lord to guide you, Molly. Your dad and I depend on God's love and wisdom to steer us on the right course."

"I pray, but doubts come anyway. Brent and I haven't known each other long, but I felt a connection soon after we met. Something about him touched me. Underneath his bravado, I saw his vulnerability, and it didn't turn me off. I loved the honesty I saw." She drew back and looked into her mother's eyes. "Don't think he's weak. He's strong in many ways, and he's kind. He makes me laugh, and he —"

Her mother pressed her finger against Molly's lips. "That's what love is, Molly. You feel it in your heart. Your spirit sings. Time isn't an issue. How long you've known each other doesn't matter. When God brings two people together to find love, our senses open to receive it. Accept the gift. Yes, be careful, but work toward it if it's your heart's desire."

Heart's desire. "I'd be empty without him."

"I think so. Enjoy the journey, Molly. I know you're impetuous, and that's frightening when it comes to love, but don't second-guess it. Let it happen. If it's the Lord's will, you'll grow in the relationship. You can't if you don't give it a chance."

Her tender look chased away Molly's concern. Time was the answer.

CHAPTER TWELVE

Brent gave the steaks another check and slid onto the picnic bench, half listening to his dad and Mr. Manning and half irritated that the steaks were going to end up overdone. He eyed the doorway again and drew in a long breath as he rose. Brent headed back to the barbecue and slid the steaks onto the plate he had waiting. He'd rather have lukewarm steaks than tough.

"Here they are," Morris said in his booming voice.

Balancing the platter, Brent looked toward the door and noticed a thoughtful expression on Molly's face. It sent a prickle down his arms. He could only guess her mother and she had been talking, but about what?

Mrs. Manning smiled at Brent's dad as she set the large platter of corn in front of him. He let out a laugh and said something that was covered by Rocket's yips as he watched the food heading his way.

While trying to shush Rocket, Brent carried the steak to the table. "The dog's next lesson would be not begging while they ate. I think Randy's been slipping him people food."

"No way," Randy said, pointing to the ground. "Rocket, down."

Rocket eyed him a minute and then lay on the grass, one eye watching the activity at the table.

The Mannings folded their hands, and Brent followed, hoping his father caught on before he grabbed corn from the platter. Mr. Manning looked at Brent. "Would you say the blessing?"

Brent's heart stopped. Say the blessing? He and prayer had been at odds until recently, and to say a prayer out loud — A knot in his chest, Brent peered at Molly's father. "Sure." The word bolted from his mouth, and he sent up a short prayer for the Lord to give him words. The paradox almost made him chuckle.

He wove his fingers together and bowed his head. Words weighed in his mind, and he sorted them. "Heavenly Father, we thank You for this . . . fellowship and for . . . for Your blessings. We ask You to bless this food to our bodies and —" He swallowed. And what? "And focus our hearts on You. Amen."

247

Everyone added an amen. Even his father's voice rumbled beneath the others. When Brent's gaze swept the table, Molly seemed to study him. Their eyes connected, and her surprise melted to a tender grin. His lungs pulled in air, and the knot in his chest vanished.

With his tension eased, Brent motioned to the food. "Enjoy, before it gets cold."

"I dropped by the other day and was amazed to see the progress." His dad selected an ear of corn and cut a pat of butter from the plate. "What do you think of the building, Art?"

Brent waited, anxious to hear his response.

"Wonderful. Molly's done a great job of using the space well, I thought." His proud gaze sought Molly's. "I know all of you have helped, and I thank you for the support you've given her."

Brent appreciated her father's enthusiasm. "No need to thank us. Molly's a persuasive woman." The salad reached him, and everyone chuckled as he spooned some into his bowl.

"You've noticed that," Art said, giving Molly a wink. "Since you've mentioned the building, we'll start painting next week." He directed his attention toward Brent. "We could use help if anyone has spare time.

We'll be working all day."

"I'll drop by after work and —"

"Daddy." Molly's expression showed her embarrassment. "They've done enough. We have plenty of help."

"I'm sure Brent will pitch in if he can." Her father's direct look connected with Brent's.

He hated painting, but the opportunity to spend time with Molly outshone the negative. Though his head battled his heart, Brent needed time to talk with her.

The conversation waned as they passed around the dishes and began to eat, except for comments about Flo's tasty potato salad and the tender steak. Brent doubted that. In the unusual silence, he'd just taken a juicy bite from the ear of corn when Molly's mother broke the silence with her startling questions.

"Morris, where do you attend worship?"

The question flew out of nowhere, and Brent sucked in a corn kernel and choked. He tried to regain his composure as he grasped his water and swallowed a gulp.

Molly flinched, and her hand flew up as if she thought she could catch the words. Her gaze flew to Brent's, her cheeks coloring to pink. "Mom, I'm not sure —"

"I hate to admit it, but my church attendance has fallen off since my wife died." Brent's father lifted his fork as if it were a pointer. "But that's not a good excuse, is it, Flo? Our family used to attend Hope Community Church, but it's been a while."

Brent turned to ice, expecting Molly's mother to confront him.

"Well then," her mother said, "wouldn't it be nice if we attended worship together? Molly attends Lighthouse Christian Church. We could all go there." She turned to Molly. "What time is the service tomorrow?"

Art patted his wife's arm. "Flo, you're putting these people on the spot."

"Not at all."

His dad's response turned all eyes on Brent. "That's fine with me."

"Then it's settled." Flo clapped her hands together, grabbed her fork and knife and cut into the steak.

Brent followed the slice of her knife and for a moment felt as if it were his neck. Then a small voice inside him whispered, "Welcome home."

Brent waited beside his car while Randy found stones on the asphalt and flipped them into the grass. Typical kid. He looked at the church, still feeling overwhelmed that he'd found himself here this morning, but something had moved Molly's mother to invite them. After he'd agreed to join Molly's family, he'd realized that the invitation had been God's doing. He'd been dealing with his faltering faith far too long, and since meeting Molly, an unexpected urge had him wanting to make restitution.

Still, his grudge with the Lord clung to him like gum on a shoe. No matter how hard he tried to scrape it off, sticky pieces still held fast. But he knew God could be very persistent.

Brent waited, and when his father's car rolled into a nearby parking space, Randy tossed the last of his stones in one handful and sprinted to his side. The boy had more energy than Brent ever remembered having.

The three of them headed for the entrance, and Brent took the steps ahead of his dad, wanting to rid himself of the anxious feeling. As soon as he stepped through the doorway, Molly waited in the entrance, a troubled expression on her face.

She stepped forward. "You came."

"Did you think I wouldn't?"

"I figured it would serve my mother right if . . ." She closed her eyes, then opened them. "I can't believe I sound so vindictive."

Before he could respond, his father loomed beside them with Randy tugging on his suit jacket, bugging to go inside.

Molly shifted to his father's side. "I apologize for my mother's pressure, but I'm so pleased you came."

His dad grasped her hand and held it. "Never apologize for someone wanting to share the Lord with others. Your mother has done me a service. I've been delinquent about putting God in my life, and today could be a new beginning." He let go of her hand as he eyed Brent. "I'll let my son speak for himself."

Brent tried to read his father's tone. Failing, he slipped his arm around Molly's shoulder. "I'm fine with this."

She gave him a questioning look. "Really."

He lowered his arm and caught her hand in his. "We'd better get inside."

"Finally," Randy said, jiggling at the doorway.

Randy and his dad led the way while Brent and Molly walked behind. Randy's eagerness was infectious, and Brent's steps felt weighted by the awareness that this might be the first time the boy had been inside a church.

Brent's father and Randy slid into the seats beside the Mannings, and Brent motioned to Molly to go ahead. When he sat, he gazed down the row, sensing God's jubilation that He'd finally gotten him back to church. Adding to the welcome feeling, Brent looked ahead at the summer sun seeping through the windows and peppering golden splotches along the carpet.

He grinned at Molly, his turmoil soothed by the music and Molly's warm look. He tried to follow the hymn. A new one to him, Brent muttered the song, hoping people around him would cover his voice. As his nervousness subsided, he focused on the single stained-glass window in front of him, a lighthouse standing tall and strong while being lashed by stormy seas. The Lord is my refuge. The words filled his mind.

The preacher strode to the platform, his Bible spread open. "If you are sinless, please raise your hand."

Brent shifted his eyes in one direction, then another. No one moved.

The preacher scanned the worshipers. "I assume, then, that you're all sinners, as I am."

A muscle ticked in Brent's jaw, and he listened to those around him muttering their yeses and amens.

"None of us have escaped sin."

The message struck Brent's thoughts.

"We are guilty and condemned."

Brent knew that. He'd breathed the sentiment all his life.

"But through God's mercy, we are all forgiven. He sees us clothed in white raiment, pure and perfect, in His eyes."

Brent winced at the image. No one would ever think of him as pure and perfect. No one. His knee bounced, and Brent pressed his hand against it to stop the agitation, but the turmoil stirred his mind. How could he ever think Molly would love him? He was too flawed.

"Unbelievers can't understand our thinking. They believe we are foolish. We are deluded and led astray by fables. But those of us who know our Father understand His unending love, forgiveness and mercy." He raised the Bible aloft. "We know the truth from scripture." He lowered the Bible and embraced it. "Though we love the Lord and praise Him, we continue to open ourselves to sin and doubts . . ."

Brent squirmed against the seat, sensing the man had read his mind.

Molly glanced his way, her eyes questioning.

His mind drifted from the message to his own situation. Could he ever let go of the guilt he felt for Randall's death? If he uttered the emotion, most people would shake their heads at his foolishness, but it was all too real for him. Molly would tell him to give it to the Lord. Brent had been taught that God answers prayer, but the Lord had ignored his.

Hearing his own heavy breathing, Brent tried to calm himself. He lowered his head, longing for the Lord to release the baggage he'd carried for too many years.

"From the New Life Bible, Isaiah 30:18," the pastor said, pulling Brent from his thoughts. " 'So the Lord wants to show you kindness. He waits on high to have loving-pity on you. For the Lord is a God of what is right and fair. And good will come to all that hope in Him.' "

The message struck him again. God is right and fair. He feels pity for people's earthly struggles, and He has goodwill for those who believe. Faith. Had his faith weakened beyond repair? No. Brent wanted God's goodwill. The hairs on his arms prickled. God gave His love freely. All Brent had to do is reach out and take it.

His hand moved to Molly's. She looked into his eyes, and he sensed she saw what he felt — something indefinable, but a kind of awareness he'd never experienced before.

Molly's fingers wound through his, her

warm palm pulsating against his.

Faith is what he needed. The Bible said faith could move mountains. The logic of that cut through him. How could he believe with confidence when he'd drifted so far from his faith? Molly's answer repeated in his mind. "Things happen in God's time, not ours."

God's time. Wait on the Lord. The words pierced his heavy thoughts.

The pastor's voice jutted into Brent's consciousness.

"When you doubt and waver —" he held the Bible above his head, his other hand over his heart "— Our God knows the truth. He knows our struggles and our regrets. He hears us crying out to Him." He lowered the Bible and extended it toward the worshipers. "It's right here in Scripture. " *We will be confident when we stand before the Lord, even if our hearts condemn us. For God is greater than our hearts, and He knows everything.*' Be confident. God knows your heart."

The scripture washed over him like baptism, like the sun sprinkling through the window. Molly's words pounded in his temple. "It's not on the outside. It's what's in the heart." Molly and God were on the same page.

A deep need rolled over him. He and Molly had to talk. If he had his way, he would escape with her after church, but with her parents' visit, suggesting such a thing would be out of the question. Once again, he'd wait.

The pungent scent of paint permeated the building. Molly stood in the doorway of her office, admiring the soft coral color she'd selected, like the beginning of a sunset and the beginning of her new endeavor to save the lives of faithful animals who only needed a good home. She'd stained the wooden shelving a warm oak that blended well with the walls, and all she needed now was furniture to complete the room.

Her fingers itched to finish the renovations and turn the building into a thriving shelter for the pets. She and Steph would work well together with the doggie day care in the back and her shelter in the front. Perfect for both.

She gave the office a sweeping gaze, pride puffing her chest, then strode into the waiting room, looking more welcoming with its copper-colored walls. She pictured families waiting, anxious to adopt a dog or sadly to give up pets they could no longer care for.

Voices echoed down the hallway, her

mother and Steph chatting as they painted in the large back room. Her parents had been at the job all day with only a quick break for fast food. Love burst inside over their sacrifice.

Having the building loaned to her without cost was another blessing, and Brent was so much a part of it. He'd settled into her world and into her heart. She'd never cared for any man as she did for him. And the realization had come to her suddenly, like a ray of sunshine that swept through the doorway and warmed her.

Yet always her nagging concern dispelled the warmth. She longed for Brent to love God with all his heart. Molly's heart skipped a beat. If she had the assurance, she could open herself to a meaningful relationship with him. She could tell him about her teen years, and God willing, their relationship could grow more deeply.

Their Fourth of July barbecue came to mind. She'd monitored her irritation and avoided pouncing on her mother for manipulating Brent and his father to attend worship, but her mother had been right. During worship, Molly had looked in Brent's eyes, and instead of a deep troubled ocean, she'd witnessed a sparkling, deep blue sea. Though they hadn't had a chance to talk, she prayed that something wonderful had happened that day.

She leaned against the office doorjamb and closed her eyes, thanking God for that amazing moment on Sunday, and then amended her prayer. *Thank you, Lord, for a mother who knows how to move a mountain.*

Faith. Things happened with faith, not worry. She'd never changed a thing with worry or fear of failure.

"Sleeping?"

Molly's eyes flew open and connected with Brent's. Time stood still as she untangled herself from her thoughts. "What are you doing here?" She noticed his pair of old faded jeans and a well-worn T-shirt, something she'd never seen him in before. "Don't tell me you're here to paint."

He glanced down the hallway and then drew her into his arms. "Okay, I won't say a word."

Brent's playfulness delighted her. "You're in a good mood."

"I am." His smile weakened. "But I have things we need to talk about." He glanced toward the back of the building. "But I don't want to be interrupted."

His eyes searched hers, warping the light-heartedness she'd experience only a moment earlier. Now everything seemed like a nebulous mess. "I'll think of something."

Brent didn't move, his gaze still clinging to hers. As if a light came on, he nodded and then lowered his arms and stepped around her to the office doorway. "I like the color." He glanced back at her. Before she realized, he'd drawn her into the room and into his arms.

"You look worried, Molly. Don't be." His hand reached up to brush a few wispy hairs from her cheek. "I've been doing a lot of thinking . . . and soul-searching."

Soul-searching. No words came that weren't packed with emotion . . . and hope.

His gaze deepened. Her arms moved on their own and wrapped around him. His lips met hers, gentle and cautious, sending chills down her spine. He drew her into an embrace, and she gave him an answer with her lips, languishing in the sweet, heady emotions so new to her.

"Oops."

Brent jerked backward with the speed of a wildcat while Molly grappled beside him to get her bearings.

"Steph, you scared me to death." Molly's lips tingled from the glorious kiss.

"Sorry. I didn't mean to interrupt." While Steph expressed her apology, her face appeared to battle against a grin.

Molly ran her fingers through her hair. "We were talking about —"

Steph's hand flew up to stop her. "You don't have to explain."

Brent seemed to have gathered his wits. He backed a few steps toward the door. "I need to offer my services to the paint crew in the back." He bolted through the doorway.

With Brent's departure, Steph burst into laughter and opened her arms. "I'm so happy for you." She gave Molly a bear hug, her giggles echoing in Molly's ear.

"It wasn't what it looked like."

Steph's eyes widened while a silly expression spread on her face. "Really? It definitely looked like a kiss to me, but then I haven't been kissed in so long maybe I'm confused."

A shot of guilt charged through Molly, thinking of Steph's troubled past. "Yes, he kissed me, but it —"

"Come on, Molly." Steph's playful expression had faded to disbelief. "How long are you going to try to convince everyone, including yourself, that you don't have feelings for the guy?"

"I have feelings — amazing feelings. I'm just confused."

"I'd give an arm to have that problem."

Molly rested her hand on Steph's shoulder. "No, you wouldn't." She managed a grin without fooling Steph.

"You make problems when they're not there. You should have lived my life."

Steph's comment knocked the wind out of her. "You're right. I'm sorry." Steph's difficult marriage and her husband's suicide swept through her mind.

"You don't have to be sorry." Steph opened her arms and gave her a hug. "You need to accept what's happening. Enjoy it. And you need to communicate with Brent. It's vital. That's when I knew Doug and I were in deep trouble. We stopped talking."

"Brent wants us to get away and talk. He just asked me."

"Do it."

"I'm nervous."

"Why?"

"He went to church with us Sunday with Mom's coercion. Now he wants to talk, and I'm so afraid. What if he says what I can't bear to hear?"

"You always talk about the importance of faith, Molly. Where's yours?"

"Floundering."

"If you want to move a mountain, you have to believe you can do it. That's faith, isn't it?"

Her eyes met Steph's. "I need to pray and

let it go."

"See? You've solved the problem already." She took a step backward. "Find a way to talk, and now I need to take off. It dawned on me that I forgot to feed Fred."

"Really?" She dangled a carrot. "I thought maybe we could go shopping."

"Shopping?" Steph's eyes brightened.

"Thrift shops. I need furniture for the waiting room and a desk for my office, and you know my ideas for the dogs' rooms."

Her face pinched. "I hope your brilliant idea will pass inspection."

Molly ignored her sarcasm and jammed her clenched fists onto her hips. "I know you hate the idea, but I'm doing it anyway and taking my chances."

Steph peered at her as she shook her head. "Stubborn."

"But look where it got me." She motioned down the hall. "I want to show the inspector that it works, and how it makes the dogs happy."

Rolling her eyes, Steph gave her a "what can I say?" shrug. "Thanks for the invite. You know me and shopping, but I really need to get home."

So much for dangling the carrot, but her refusal gave Molly a great idea. "All right. I don't want you to starve poor old Fred."

She grinned. "I'll walk you to the back." Molly darted into the office and grabbed her shoulder bag from a shelf and headed down the hallway with Steph.

The odor of paint grew stronger as she passed the dog pens, small rooms with Dutch doors — so different from cages — but it was important to her.

Her heart swelled with gratefulness, witnessing her father rolling the paint while her mother brushed on the trim. She adored them.

Her mother looked over her shoulder. "We'll be done soon. Just a little trim work left."

"Good news."

Her parents halted to say goodbye to Steph while Molly tried to get Brent's attention.

Finally, he gave her a questioning look.

She waited until she heard the crunch of Steph's tires on the driveway. "I asked Steph to go with me to the Salvation Army Thrift Shop, but she can't. So maybe Brent could go since you're about finished here." She turned to Brent. "How about it?"

He grinned and gave her a wink. "Shopping? If it'll help."

His playing-it-cool response tickled her. Her gaze shifted from her mother to her dad. "You won't mind if Brent and I check out furniture, would you?"

Her dad pounded the lid onto the paint can and straightened. "Hang on a minute. I'll wash up and go with you. If you buy something big, I can help carry —"

Molly's hand shot in the air. "No, Dad. Thanks, but you and Mom have done enough. I'll just have them hold it until tomorrow. I'll rent a trailer." She walked over and gave her dad a one-armed hug, avoiding his paint splotches. "Why don't you and Mom go out to dinner? On me. You've earned it. Brent and I can catch dinner later."

Her mother turned toward her, the paintbrush suspended. "Why shop now? It's late."

Would they never catch on? "The store's open until nine. They have lots of inexpensive furniture. I'm anxious to see what they have."

Her father gave an approving grin while her mother shrugged. "Okay, but did you look at yourself in the mirror? You have paint splattered on your top."

Molly eyed her paint-splotched jeans and baggy T-shirt. She did look a mess. She cringed. Brent had kissed her looking like that. The memory swished over her, her lips tingling with the recollection. She lifted her chin. "They don't care at the thrift shop. It's not as if I'm going to Nordstrom." She added a grin.

Brent chuckled as he studied her face. "You do have a couple of medium-green freckles on your cheek." He used his finger to scratch away the paint.

Molly wanted to kiss him, but she managed to turn away and wave goodbye to her parents as Brent headed out the door. She made her escape and slipped into his car. "Alone at last."

He leaned toward her and kissed the tip of her nose. "Perfect."

She nodded. Perfect is just the way she liked it.

CHAPTER THIRTEEN

Inside the thrift store, Brent followed Molly through the furniture section and though she pointed at chairs and tables as possible choices, he could see her mind wasn't on shopping. His suggestion to shop first and eat later had been a dumb idea.

Though he'd tried to catch Molly's eye, she hadn't looked at him for the past few minutes. Her mind obviously wasn't on him or the furniture.

She tugged at his heart. Dressed in her paint-splattered clothes, she still looked beautiful to him. Her oval face with creamy skin glowed with the summer's touch. Her eyes flashed the same gold tones in her hair. Beneath all the outer layers lay a spirit and heart filled with love and generosity. She was stubborn, yes. Prideful in ways. Determined, which wasn't all bad. And amazing.

Brent caught up with her and wove his

fingers through hers. "Stupid idea, wasn't it?"

A blank look shaded her face, then light broke. "You mean waiting to talk."

"I thought we could shop first so we didn't have to worry about the store closing, but I can't focus on anything." He glanced around the quiet store. Only one clerk at the late hour and a handful of customers, mainly in the clothing areas. "What do you say we try out some of these chairs?" He squeezed her hand. "Let's talk."

Relief spread across her face. "Please. I'm miserable."

His breath hitched. "I told you not to worry." He steered her to the leatherlike love seat she'd admired, and he sat beside her. When he looked at her, he turned to ice. "I'm not sure where to start, Molly. When I try to organize my thoughts, they get muddled. So many things connect." He rested his arms on his knees lowered his face in his hands to think.

Molly shifted. "Are you okay?"

He could hear the old fear gaining momentum in her voice. He raised his head and looked into her eyes. "Do I start with the chicken or the egg?"

Molly's eyes shifted upward, as if in thought. She looked at him. "Start with the chicken."

"Chicken." He rubbed his cheek. Which chicken? He'd struggled with so many. He managed a grin.

Her color heightened. "Start with the worship service on Sunday. Something happened."

He knew she'd noticed his squirming during the service. Brent shifted to face her. "Things you've said to me struck me that day." His mind flew back to the service — the music, the scripture, the message. "The pastor's sermon validated so much you've tried to tell me, and I felt as if a door opened."

She leaned forward, her look intense. "A good door?"

Her concern swept over him. "Awareness. Understanding. Yes, a good door."

Her distress melted into a tender expression. "Understanding about what?"

The anxious tone in her voice darted through Brent's chest. "About what you've said, and I've come to one important conclusion — I don't understand God."

Her eyes flashed. "No one does. If we could totally understand the Lord, we'd be God, and we're not. But we are His children and we trust Him."

"And that's the crux of my problem. I

don't trust well."

A customer passed, giving them a curious look before moving on. They sat in silence a moment until the man was out of earshot.

Molly leaned closer. "But . . . but you trusted me. You gave me the benefit of the doubt on using your building for the shelter, and you convinced the board to agree. That's trust."

He had trusted her. "But do I trust God?"

"Only you know that, Brent, and if you're asking the question, then you must believe God is real. It wouldn't be a question otherwise."

He shrank into the cushion, startled by the realization. He'd prayed to God. Would he pray to someone or something unreal? That would be absurd.

Molly leaned even closer. "When the Lord gets into your heart, He stays there, Brent. You can slam the lid on his presence, but He's still there."

"Then why doesn't He hear my prayers, Molly? That's what I need to understand."

Her back straightened. "He hears them. He's your heavenly Father. He doesn't always say yes to us, just like our own fathers. Sometimes He says no."

As if a rock struck him, Brent jolted with memories of his own father. It was all too familiar.

Molly's hand slipped from his, and she brushed back a few strands of loosened hair. "We can't see the future. We don't know the ramifications of our wants. Let's say you begged your father for a car. He bought you one and you got in an accident and were badly injured or you hurt someone else in an accident. If your dad could see into the future, he would have said no."

It made sense, but he still didn't like it. He thought of Randy, who'd been bugging him for a bike. Though he hadn't given Randy an answer, he'd planned on answering by surprising him with a bicycle for his birthday. That's the kind of father Brent had always wanted.

He looked at Molly's expectant expression. "I get your point."

She glanced toward the clerk at the checkout station and then swung back. "But you can still trust God to hear your prayers and answer yes or no in His time."

"I've heard you say this before, Molly. I've been waiting a lifetime."

"I don't like to wait, either, but we all have to sometimes. God sees the big picture."

"Then are you saying if I have trust I also have faith?"

She lowered her head, and her silence

made him nervous. His jaw tightened, confused by her reaction.

When Molly lifted her head, she faced him with a serious expression. "They're different."

"Different? Trust and faith. I think they're the same."

She shook her head. "Trust is confidence. If I say I'll do something, you can trust me to do it." Her expression grew weightier. "Faith is confidence plus truth."

"Truth?"

"It's believing that something is true even though it might not be logical to many people. It's believing in something you can't prove but you know it. It goes deeper than seeing it with your eyes or holding it in your hand."

Brent sorted through her statement. "In other words, God. Believing that God is real and that He will do all the things He promises."

A beautiful smile brightened her face.

"I can't hold God in my hand, but I can hold Him in my heart."

Tears brimmed her eyes, and the air escaped Brent's lungs. He wanted to draw Molly into his arms and kiss her tears away — kiss away all her fears until his own messed-up thinking had been piled on the street for trash pickup. "I didn't mean to make you sad."

She brushed the mist from her eyes. "I'm not sad. I'm thrilled. You get it."

"And I believe it, Molly, but I'm a baby taking his first steps."

She clasped her hand in his, her warmth firing his longing to let her know how much he cared. "You can lean on God and on me."

Her sweetness touched him. His other problem sank into the mire. He didn't want to lose the moment. He pushed away the past. The more he delved into his long-time bitterness, the more ridiculous it became. He'd always envisioned God as vindictive, as a God who got even and punished, an Old Testament God who fired brimstone on cities and turned sinners into pillars of salt. He'd forgotten the loving mercy, the promised forgiveness and Jesus' outstretched arms that offered to carry his burdens.

Tonight Brent clung to those promises. He could be a role model for Randy and forgive his father. And he could love. Molly had taught him that.

Brent rose. He had much more to say, but this wasn't the place. "Let's make some decision. I'm starving."

She laughed, and the sound lifted the weight from his shoulders. What would he do without her now that she'd charged into his life?

"It's wonderful." Molly brushed tears from her eyes as she wandered through the shelter, admiring the new look with all the furniture she and Brent had selected. Her office held other purchases she'd previously ordered from an office supply store — a desk, desk chair, file cabinet and computer equipment.

The leatherlike chairs and love seat from the thrift shop fit her needs in the waiting room. She'd added a couple of tables and a lamp. One table held brochures and information about adoption and caring for animals. Her heart soared, experiencing her long-awaited dream coming true.

"You've done wonders." Brent slipped his arm around her shoulders. "I wouldn't recognize the old factory with all this paint and even pictures on the walls."

She bought frames and used calendar photos of dogs to create an eclectic wall arrangement.

Footsteps from the hallway drew nearer, and Molly turned as her mother stepped into the waiting room, clapping her hands together as if beating off dust. "Everything looks great." She motioned down the hall.

"Brent, did you see the dog pens?"

"Not since you fancied them up." He linked his arm to her mother's and followed her down the hall.

Molly took a final look at the waiting room, glanced into her office and the medical room where the volunteer veterinarians would give shots and spay and neuter dogs and then followed them to the cubicles, anxious to approve the final preparations for the inspector.

Her nerves knotted. Today was the day. Approval or no approval. Then she'd have to change or fix whatever they didn't like. She glanced at her watch, fearing they'd arrive before Steph. She'd promised to come and bring Fred to let him wander around and approve the setup. She chuckled at the idea of a dog sanctioning the facility. But she trusted good old Fred.

She reached Brent and her mom, peering into one of the small rooms. Brent had agreed with Steph. He thought she was taking a chance on the setup, too.

She bustled between them. "What do you think? Everything can be sanitized. I don't see how they can complain that I'm not using cages."

Brent arched a brow. "Cages are common. This is unorthodox, but then so is the

275

person who thought of it."

Molly scanned his face, hoping he'd been joking. He gave her a playful wink, and she nestled closer, wishing for a moment they were alone. She longed to kiss him. Brent slid his arm around her back as they moved down the aisle, looking at each cubicle and making general comments about her homey additions — pictures on the wall and a box holding doggie toys. She'd tried to think of everything to make the dogs feel loved.

Loved. Since their talk a few days earlier, she'd allowed herself to dream about love. She'd allowed her hopes to take wing, soaring into the blue sky and leaving her worries behind. Brent had made a faith commitment. He'd taken steps, small ones but steps nonetheless. Now she had to move forward with her own confession.

Her father called from the back, and her mother hurried away. When she gazed up at Brent, he kissed the tip of her nose. "Congratulations, Molly. This might be unorthodox, but it reflects your love for the animals. You've made it their home."

The need to kiss him overpowered her inspection worries, and she tiptoed to reach his mouth.

"I'm here." Steph's voice bounced in her

ear along with Fred's nails clicking on the tile.

Molly halted her momentum and pulled her heels to the floor. "You made it."

"Did you think I wouldn't?" She arched one eyebrow. "And for some reason, I always appear at the most interesting times." A smile stole to her face.

Molly sent her a coy look. "I refuse to make excuses this time."

Brent turned his neck from Molly to Steph and back again, as if befuddled by their conversation. Molly decided to leave him in the dark for now. Only Steph had seen her on tiptoes.

Molly motioned toward the pen and opened the door. "Let Fred go inside. I want to see what he does."

Steph detached his leash, and Fred, nose to the ground, smelled his way into the new retreat. He sniffed the scatter rug and the forest-toned beanbag cushion in the corner, salvaged probably from someone's basement to end up at the thrift shop.

Steph grinned over the top of the Dutch door. "Do you like it, Fred?"

He pawed at the beanbag and proceeded to climb on top and curl up.

The heat of excitement burst on Molly's face. "That's what I wanted to see."

"Molly."

Her dad's voice captured her attention. She turned and saw a stranger with him. The man extended his hand. "I'm Ernie Schultz from the Department of Agriculture . . . for the inspection."

Molly ran her moist palm over her jeans and shook his hand. "Thanks for coming." Before she could say any more, he'd already begun to eye the dog cubicles, a sour look on his face. Her pulse skittered to a throbbing in her chest.

Ernie wandered from one to the other, a permanent scowl on his face. She gave the others a frantic look while her father made a quick getaway. Brent sent her a painfully hopeful look and then stepped away, too, heading to the back, where her mother had also disappeared. So much for her support group. She swallowed the lump in her throat.

"Who do we have here?" Ernie eyed the room where Fred had made himself comfortable. Steph stood against the wall, apparently trying to stay out of the way.

"That's Fred. He's my friend's dog. He likes the setup."

Shaking his head, Ernie paced the hallway, peering into one pen, then another. "But this type of cage is —"

"It's a room."

He eyed Molly, the scowl still etched on his face. "Yes, I see it's a room. This type of facility is uncommon. It doesn't follow the conventional style of housing for the animals. It makes my job more difficult."

She saw Steph flinch with the man's comments, and she could also hear the "I told you so" bellowing in Steph's thoughts.

"I realize that, but remember, unless we find foster or adoptive homes for the animals, the dogs live here. I wanted them to feel loved and be in a homey environment. Everything we've used can be disinfected and washed."

He wandered toward the room Fred occupied as she spoke, but Molly couldn't read his expression. Her nerves tightened.

When he passed the Dutch door and stepped inside, Fred rose from the cushion and sniffed his pant leg. Ernie crouched and petted the dog's head as he studied the surroundings. "I see everything is plastic or leatherlike." He rose and touched the beanbag and then looked at the plastic bin filled with dog toys. He stepped back. "And the rugs can be washed."

"Yes. I understand the need for sanitation to keep the dogs healthy."

He rubbed his fingers down his chin.

Molly's heart thumped. "Would you like to see the rest? We have a very nice room for our visiting veterinarian."

Ernie followed her down the hall. She knew his greatest concern was where the dogs were kept, but she hoped he would see how hard they'd worked to create a quality shelter. He asked a few questions as she showed him the front of the building, and when they made their way to the back, everyone, along with Fred, was gathered in a small circle, their faces etched with worry. So was Molly's.

"This area is for inside play and exercise on inclement days. Otherwise we have a fenced yard where the dogs can be outside for playtime."

He made a note on his clipboard, and when she looked up, Molly was surprised to see Morris coming through the door. He lifted a hand in greeting and then pulled Brent to the side of the room while her curiosity got the better of her.

Ernie stood a moment, checking boxes and scribbling notes on the form. "Water?"

"Yes. We have water." The inane response made her giddy, and Molly released an embarrassing giggle. "Naturally." She motioned for him to follow and she showed him their work room and storage area. "We have large water dishes for each room."

Ernie made another check on the form, tucked the pencil back into his shirt pocket and strode back down the hall without comment.

Molly bit her lip, her mind spinning out of control, tears pushing behind her eyes. What would she do if he didn't approve the shelter?

When they reached the others, Morris's voice split the silence. "This is a wonderful shelter, you agree." Not a question, but a firm statement.

Molly flinched, waiting to hear what Ernie had to say.

He eyed Morris without comment.

"I own this building." Morris extended his hand toward Ernie. "Morris Runyan."

Ernie's eyebrows shot up as he shook Morris's hand and introduced himself. "Miss Manning is leasing from you?"

"No, we've given her the use of the building. We have faith in her and the shelter. Her proposal went before our board of directors at Runyan Industrial Tool Corporation and was accepted." Morris shifted his sturdy frame closer to Ernie. "When will Molly receive approval? Today, or will she be notified at a later date?"

Molly's eyes widen, seeing Morris's tack.

No wonder the Runyan board approved her proposal.

Ernie clutched the clipboard against his chest. "Miss Manning will receive an official report through the mail."

Morris arched a heavy eyebrow. "But you make the decision."

"Well . . . yes."

"Then what is that decision? Approval, I assume."

Ernie stammered a moment. "Yes. She meets all requirements, although the cages are unorthodox."

Morris gripped Ernie's shoulder. "And that's why we supported Molly's proposal with enthusiasm. She truly cares about the animals. This isn't a scheme to make money but a devotion to providing homes for the abandoned dogs." His gaze captured Molly's. "I admire anyone who unselfishly tries to improve the world."

Ernie nodded. "Yes. I can see she's put a lot of work into this shelter. It's very . . . homey."

"Good." Morris gave him a genial slap on the back. "Molly can move ahead then with finalizing her plans to open."

Ernie edged toward the door. "She'll receive her permit in the mail in a couple of days."

"Wonderful." Morris's voice boomed with such force that Molly jumped.

The poor man skittered through the door and made a quick getaway.

Molly's pulse skipped and then accelerated again. Approval. The seed of a dream had blossomed into reality. "Morris, thank you so much."

Although Brent smiled, beneath it Molly sensed his irritation at his father's forceful ploy. Molly didn't approve, either, but today she wanted to give Morris a big kiss on the cheek. Why Morris had become so gung ho escaped her, but she accepted the gift as a blessing.

Morris slipped his arm around her shoulder and gave her a quick hug. "Congratulations, Molly."

"Thanks for coming." She looked at the group posed around her, their smiles still beaming. "We should celebrate."

"Great idea." Morris clapped his hands. "I'm taking everyone out to dinner tonight. What do you say?"

Molly raised her hand. "I didn't mean you should —"

"It's my pleasure." He looked toward Brent. "You set a time. I need to get moving. Randy's at my house with the housekeeper, and I'm supposed to be birthday shopping. He gave me a list."

Brent's voice cut through the air. "Don't get the bike, Dad. I already have one hidden in the garage."

Morris grinned. "Don't worry. It's a long list." He took a step toward the door before glancing back at the group. "I'll see you all tonight."

"Happy Birthday, dear Randy. Happy Birthday to you . . ."

Randy grinned, took a big breath and blew out the twelve candles.

As everyone applauded, Brent ruffled Randy's hair, realizing in another year he would have to deal with a teenager. "Let's have the cake and ice cream, and then —" he sent Randy a playful look "— we can open the rest of your gifts."

Molly pitched in to cut the cake while Randy doled out scoops of ice cream, and Brent stood back, blanketed by the feeling of family, a sensation he'd never experienced quite like this. Rain had fallen on Randy's actual birthday date, the Thursday before, but today the sun shone, making it a perfect Saturday for the celebration.

"Did everyone see my new bike?" Randy asked, plopping into a chair and dipping into the ice cream.

Molly raised her hand like a kid in school. "I did. It's beautiful. Do you know how to ride?"

Randy gave a huge nod. "I practiced yesterday." He looked over at Brent. "I'm pretty good. Right, Uncle Brent?"

Brent's chest puffed, picturing Randy's tremendous progress after the first day of struggle to master his balance. "He's doing great."

Pride heightened the glow of Randy's face. "Can I show them later?"

Brent gave him a wink. "But only after we open your other gifts."

That seemed to be agreeable with Randy.

As they enjoyed the birthday cake, the conversation shifted to the dog shelter and Molly's parents leaving the next day after worship.

Morris rose for another slice of cake. "Just a small sliver," he said, giving his belly a pat. "Did the inspection approval arrive yet?" He looked up from the cake plate toward Molly.

Her joyful expression gave the answer. "Yesterday. I felt like I'd been given the Miss America crown."

Brent's pulse kicked up a notch. Molly enthralled him. She'd become the sunshine in his world, and the awareness set him on edge. Though Molly remained guarded, he'd experienced a crack in her armor — more than a crack — a space he had wiggled through. He sensed he'd penetrated her heart, but she still remained cautious.

He'd told her about his faith, and he'd admitted feeling responsible for his brother's death, although he'd fallen short of telling her why. The day would come soon when he could let that go, too. Then he could tell her the whole truth. He'd fallen in love with her.

Fallen in love. Brent never thought he would say those words, but he didn't have to. The emotion permeated his heart and soul so deeply he ached.

Though his father had once again stepped over the line, using his power play with the inspector, Brent had assumed the shelter would pass inspection. Molly had thought of everything. His chest expanded as he admired Molly's skill and pure love that drove her to reach her dream.

One day she would make his dream come true — a dream he'd never experienced until he'd met her.

He rose and offered his guests more cake or ice cream. When everyone passed, he began gathering the plates and forks to carry to the kitchen.

But Molly moved beside and whispered near his ear. "Let me do this. You can bring in the rest of the gifts. Randy's been so good about waiting while we ate."

He grinned, recognizing Molly's excitement as much as Randy's. He retrieved the gifts from the great room and set them on the table.

Randy's face glowed. He settled himself in front of the pile, fingering the ribbons and eyeing the boxes.

When Molly hurried back from the kitchen, Randy dug into his presents — a skateboard from Molly, the knee-and-elbow pads from her parents and his father's surprise Wii console and the games software.

Randy let out a hoot. "I love it, Grand-dad. I can go bowling right here." He swung his arm back and let it fly, nearly knocking a glass off the table.

"Slow down, pal." Brent shifted forward and removed any breakable items near Randy, not wanting to squelch his enthusiasm. "We can look at that later, but first . . ." He gave Randy a subtle poke with his elbow.

Randy stood and grinned. "Thanks for all the neat presents. I've never had such a great birthday. Ever."

Molly began the applause, and everyone joined in.

He spun around toward Brent. "Can I show them the bike now?"

"Sure. Go ahead. We'll come out front in a minute."

Flo collected the gift wrap and shoved it into the waste basket, while Art and Morris carried the gifts into the family room.

Brent set a couple of coffee cups in the sink and then followed the rest toward the front door.

By the time they assembled outside, Randy had pedaled down the block. Brent stood on the grassy berm, keeping an eye on him.

Molly ambled closer and gave his arm a squeeze. "Look how much he's grown up. He's wonderful, Brent. I'm so happy to see the changes even since I met him."

Everything had changed since Molly stepped into his life. Randy adored her and even seemed happy going to church with her the past two Sundays.

While Brent watched Randy, his mind headed back to his earlier discussion with Molly. Though he still clung to some old feelings, Brent had done everything he could to forgive his father for the past. He'd even had a better understanding why God said no. But seeing the joy in Randy's face on his birthday when he was sent to the garage for the surprise bicycle made Brent wonder why the Lord didn't say yes more often.

"Whoa!"

Brent spun around, hearing Art's yell. Rocket shot past Art's legs while Brent darted forward to catch the dog, who'd obviously gotten out of the backyard. He kicked himself for not checking the gate. Randy was careless with that. "Rocket. Come!"

The dog ignored his call and raced down the sidewalk toward Randy.

Brent cupped his hands around his mouth. "Rocket!"

Molly darted after the dog.

Brent joined her, but his heart stopped when Rocket veered into the street as a car turn the corner. "Randy!" Brent headed toward them, waving his arms.

Randy waved back, then spotted Rocket. In a split second, Randy dropped his bicycle on the edge of the street and ran toward Rocket.

"Randy! A car!" Brent's voice pierced the air as he closed his eyes.

The car's brakes squealed.

Rocket darted onto the grass, and Randy flew into the air, spun twice on the hood and then plummeted to the ground.

CHAPTER FOURTEEN

Molly sat beside Brent in the hospital waiting room while Morris visited Randy in the emergency cubicle. Brent's head rested in his hands as she drew her palm across his back in soothing strokes, not knowing what else to do or say. She'd said it all. He hadn't been to blame. Kids wanted bicycles, and he'd given him one.

Though longing to see Randy, Molly had not taken a turn to go in since visitation was limited, but she knew she'd feel better if she had even a moment with him. The image of Randy flying into the air and bouncing on the car's hood turned her stomach. She shifted in the seat, trying to force her thoughts from that horrifying moment.

"I know what you said, Molly, but I feel rotten." He fell against the cushion, shaking his head. "The other day you gave me an example of not always saying yes, and it's killing me."

She drew a blank. "Example of what?"

"You said something about if a kid wanted a car and his father could look into the future and see the boy would have a serious accident, the father would say no. I keep thinking of that."

Air shot from her lungs. She had said that. Molly bit her lip, wishing she hadn't. "I guess I did, but that wasn't a premonition. It was an analogy."

"But it makes sense. God knows what's going to happen in the future. We have no idea."

Molly slipped her fingers through his. "Brent, you can't spend your life saying no because something might happen. Randy's going to be all right. After the accident, the first thing he asked was about his bicycle. You heard him. He'll be bruised, but he'll heal, and he'll be more careful from now on."

"Still, I realize what a responsibility it is to be a father. I don't think I can do the job."

"Shush. You're wonderful with Randy. I just told you that. He's matured, because you've given him attention and shown him love."

"Love I never thought I had in me."

"Because you didn't feel it when you were a child. You know your parents loved you. They just loved differently."

"I realize that now, but I didn't then." Brent pressed his free hand over their entwined fingers. "Molly, I've been wanting to tell you about something. It's one of the things that's bothered me so much of my —"

"Randy has a slight concussion and a fractured arm." Morris's voice reached them as he strode forward. "His left arm. The right would have made it worse, I suppose."

Brent's face paled. "Fractured arm."

Morris tilted his head toward the door. "Go in. They're going to set it, and they might keep him overnight. Just to be safe."

Brent shot off the chair and vanished through the doorway.

Morris crumpled into Brent's chair. "He looks okay, though. Frightened, but okay." He pressed his hand to his chest. "That gave me a scare."

"Me, too, but. I'm grateful it's nothing worse." She sent a thank-you to the Lord without hesitation. She'd nagged Him with her pleas since she'd seen the horrible accident.

Concerned about Morris's ashen complexion, Molly touched his arm. "Are you okay?"

"I'm fine." He patted her hand. "I'm not used to all this excitement." He chuckled. "And I don't want to be, either. Nice quiet evenings are enough for me."

She grinned, glad he'd maintained a sense of humor.

Morris slipped his hand into his jacket pocket and pulled out an envelope. "I planned to give you this as I was leaving the party, but this is as good a time as any." He slipped the envelope into her hand.

Molly held it, eyeing the plain white covering with her name scrawled across the front in broad strokes.

"Open it."

The command propelled her. She drew her index finger beneath the closure and tore it open. Inside, she saw a check. Her heart bucked. "What is this?"

"A gift."

"A gift?" She studied him again while he nodded toward the check.

Molly inched it from beneath the flap, afraid to look. She swallowed hard and forced her eyes downward. Her heart stopped. "I don't understand."

"You can't question a gift. No strings attached."

She looked again to make sure she hadn't misread the figure. One hundred thousand dollars. The numbers swirled in her mind. "But . . . ?"

"Molly, I've made a lot of mistakes in my life, and for once I want to do something good and unselfish."

"You'll be a partner. I'll write up a contract and —"

"Molly."

"I'll pay it back when we begin to —"

"Please do me this favor and accept the gift."

She drew the check against her chest, pressing it between her hands. "Do you know what this will do? I can get the shelter going without fear of falling on my face. I can provide homes for dogs, train them so they won't be euthanized when all I need is time to find the right home for them. It means more than you'll ever know."

He shook his head. "I know, because I've experienced something similar."

Her brow furrowed, unable to fathom what he might mean.

"You, Molly. You've been a light in my dark life, and you've given that light to my son and grandchild. You're a beacon of hope and faith. Money can't thank you enough for what you've done, but I know it will help you, and it's what I want to do."

His voice whirled through her mind. Darkness. Light. Hope. Faith. Could she have done all of that? She knew better. Morris had opened his heart and let God's light in. She'd just been there when it happened. "Does Brent know?"

"I'll tell him. He might be angry that I'm butting in again, but it'll pass."

"Can I give you a kiss on the cheek?"

"I'd be honored."

He leaned forward, and she pressed her lips on his cool skin.

"Molly?"

She twisted around and looked into Brent's bewildered eyes. "What's happening?"

"A thank-you." She slipped the check into her bag and then rose and put her arms around his shoulders. "How's Randy?"

Confusion etched his face. "He wants to see you."

She glanced at Morris, then back to Brent. "I'll just be a minute."

Morris patted the chair Molly had vacated. "Sit. I want to tell you something."

The befuddled look marked Brent's face as Molly turned and headed out the door. In a moment, Molly stood beside Randy's bed.

He opened his eyes and gave her a brave look that wrenched her heart. "I broke my arm."

"I know," she said, eyeing the splints as she brushed the hair from his forehead. His brow felt clammy. "How are you feeling?"

He gave a minute shrug. "Scared."

"Don't be. We're all out there in the waiting room, and Jesus is right here beside you."

His eyes shifted as he scanned the room. When he looked back, he gave her a faint nod. "I might have to stay here all night."

Her chest pinged. "But you'll go home tomorrow. Probably in the morning."

"Okay."

Molly gazed at his innocent face while he tried to be brave. She leaned over and kissed his flushed cheek, surprised to feel the chill of the room on his flesh. "I'll see you later."

"I love you."

His words knocked the wind from her. She blinked back her tears and uttered the words she'd longed to say. "I love you, too."

In the hallway, she lowered her face in her hands as reality rocked her. She couldn't hurt the boy. Molly couldn't even think of the possibility. She could never abandon Randy now.

She dragged herself back to the waiting

room, trying to get her emotions in check. Although knowing Randy's love for her touched her heart, her relationship with Brent still had an edge to it that she'd caused herself. He'd professed his faith — baby steps, but she knew the seed had been replanted — and he would grow and flourish in his acceptance of the Lord's promises. All her fretting and worrying had produced nothing but unhappiness. The door had been opened, the shackles of her prison broken away, and now she was free to move ahead. So what did she fear?

She stopped in the waiting room doorway, assuming Morris had told Brent about the check and expecting to see frustration on his face. She stood a moment until he noticed her. He gave her a tender grin and then rose and opened his arms. "Feel better seeing him?"

"Very much." She stepped into his embrace, realizing Morris hadn't told him. The disappointment marshaled her anxiety.

He drew back, and his inquisitive look let her know he'd sensed her tension.

Brent steered her back to the chair, and she assumed he'd head back to Randy. It would give her a chance to ask Morris why he didn't tell Brent about the check.

"Dad, why don't you go in with Randy

for a while."

Morris rose without resistance and patted Brent's shoulder, giving him a wink that bewildered Molly. As he strode into the hallway, Brent settled beside her, his look hooded.

"Are you worried?" That's the only thing she could think that would cause his guarded expression.

"No. Randy will be fine." He slipped his fingers through hers.

"He will be, and probably home tomorrow."

He seemed unsettled, and she worried he knew something about Randy she didn't.

Brent shifted to face her more fully. "I've had something I've been trying to tell you."

Panic tore through her. "Something's wrong with Randy?"

"It's not Randy." He captured her hand as he glanced at the door. "Before my dad comes back, let me get this off my chest."

She held her breath. He did know about the check.

"You know about my brother. He was a tease and enjoyed taunting me."

His brother? The unexpected topic boggled her mind.

"You know that Toby was given away because of my lack of responsibility."

"Given away? Your dad told me —"

"That was the story he told me. My dad made rash decisions. I lived with them."

"Oh, Brent."

"Let me tell you the real story." His jaw twitched as his frown deepened. "I had never expected Dad to go that far with his threats. I tried to remember to feed and water Toby, but sometimes I'd run to my room, avoiding my brother, and I'd forget."

He looked into her eyes and gave her an apologetic look.

"I'm listening." Listening, but having trouble following. Molly's thoughts had splintered with Randy, the check and now Brent's story.

"I'll get to the point."

She grimaced, fearing she'd let him see her confusion.

"My dad gave Toby to my brother to use for hunting. I lived in fear that something would happen to him. Bullets flying around. Toby was new to hunting. I resented that Dad had allowed Randall to use my dog. My brother taunted me that Toby wasn't a good retriever. He told me someone would probably shoot him, because he was so useless."

"Brent." Her hearts stood still. "He didn't."

"He said it, but no, he didn't hurt the dog. But my continual whining bugged him, and one day Randall came home from hunting and said Toby had run away. I asked my dad, and he only shrugged his shoulders. I cried for a week. I was certain that Randall had done something awful. Remember, I was younger than Randy."

Molly ached, hearing the story and imagining how any child would feel. "Your suspicion was logical. Anyone might suspect that."

"The truth was, Dad had given Toby away, and Randall took care of it, but I didn't know that until later when Randall got tired of my questions. I wanted details and probed to find out how hard he'd searched for the dog. He told me the truth and then laughed at me."

Molly's stomach knotted.

"But before I knew the truth, what kills me is I hated my brother. I prayed he'd die like I thought Toby had."

Molly's pulse raced. She knew how Randall died, and she could understand Brent's agony.

"I kept thinking how much Randall deserved a horrible death like he'd done to Toby. When I learned the truth, those prayers ended, but not the dislike for my

300

brother. Then years later it happened. Randy was shot —"

"I know how Randall died." She grasped both his hands in hers. "You mean all these years you thought God had finally answered your prayers."

"You always tell me it's in His time, Molly."

She swallowed the lump in her throat. "God has a plan for all His children, and He knows when they need to leave the earth. He doesn't answer children's confused prayers like that."

"I realize that now, but then, it grew into a mountain. I wanted you to understand why I was a mess when you met me. I'd clung to that twisted thinking for so long it had become real. I even disliked pets because of it."

"We do those things to ourselves." Molly's knotted stomach turned upside down. "We all have delusions, and we all have secrets. I have mine."

Brent's head jerked upward, his eyes flashing disbelief. "You?"

She nodded. "I had a long talk with my mother about one delusion I had, but I have something else I need to tell you about my teen years."

"Your teen years?"

She nodded and then glanced toward the doorway, praying she had enough time before Morris returned.

A frown darkened his face while she thought back to those days at the end of her senior year. "I messed up badly in my senior year. It started the summer before. My dream was to be a veterinarian. That's all I wanted, and you know me — what I want, I get."

Brent's eyes searched her face.

"Up to then my grades were excellent. A 4.0. I'd been a good student. I met my parents expectations, but near the end of my junior year, I rebelled. Many kids from my class were drinking, trying drugs, becoming promiscuous. I'd begun to feel like an outcast. I hadn't experienced anything. In the summer, I tossed my faith out the door and joined in."

She looked at Brent's questioning face and barreled ahead. "I'd had a few drinks at parties, at first, pretending I'd had more than I'd really had. You know, just to feel I was one of the gang." She faltered, hating to continue.

Brent nodded. "I understand, Molly."

"Then it changed. The night before the college tests we'd had a party. I drank too much that night, and on the way home, the guy pulled onto a dark side street and . . ." She looked into his anxious face. "You know the rest."

Brent slipped his fingers through hers. "Molly, we all make mistakes."

"There's more."

His eyes searched hers. "You messed up the tests.

She nodded, blinking back tears and garnering courage to finish the story. "Yes. Veterinary programs are few, and acceptance is impossible without being at the top."

"And you didn't make it."

"It wasn't only that, Brent. I thought I was pregnant. I panicked. I felt dirty and awful. I thought of abortion, but I knew I couldn't do that. By then I realized that I'd not only devastated my parents, but I'd turned my back on God."

He cupped her hand in both of his. "What did you do?"

"I wasn't pregnant. My folks were startled, but they stood by me, even when they thought it was true. It changed my life. From that day on, I promised myself I'd never lose my concentration on a dream, and I turned my back on men. I couldn't trust them or me."

Moisture rimmed Brent's eyes. "You suffered too long with this. Give it to the Lord."

Her heart soared. "I never have . . . until you came along."

Brent's hand tensed beneath hers. She lifted her eyes to his. "And I'm glad you did. I would have lost something wonderful."

"I'm glad to hear you say that." He kissed her fingers. "I'm glad you came along. You've made me whole again, and you've given me faith. I'd be lost without you, Molly. I'm sorry you had to go through what you did, but you grew from it, and it drew you closer to God."

"It did that. That's when I couldn't settle for anything less than the best I could be." Her comment triggered another thought. "I mentioned delusion, and let me tell you one I lived with for so many years." She began her story, relating the recent talk she'd had with her mother. "I was looking for a fairy tale. Something that doesn't exist. Now I know the truth — that a relationship is based on the ability to cherish the positives and handle the negatives in a positive way."

Brent's serious expression faded to a tender grin. "That's you, Molly. Absolutely optimistic."

"It's the only way to be."

He squeezed her hand. "I'm glad we both opened up, Molly. I don't want there to be any secrets between us."

"Never again. Promise."

He slipped his arm around her shoulders. "Promise."

Molly sat in silence, Brent's arm holding her close, their thoughts somewhere else until she lifted her gaze. "Did your father tell you about the check?"

"He did."

Hearing his tone, her concern edged away. "And you approve? It's okay?"

"He explained, and I'm all for it. Dad has a hard time expressing himself without using money as the reward. It's his gift for all you've done for Randy and for me. You've changed us, Molly."

She placed her palm against his cheek. "It wasn't me, Brent. You changed yourself."

"But with your help . . . and the Lord's."

His words assured her that God was at work. "I wonder where your dad is."

He gave her hand a squeeze and sent her a loving smile. "Don't worry. I'm guessing they're setting Randy's arm about now."

The image of Randy, struggling to be brave and his sweet "I love you" struck her again. "I can't help but think of how Randy looked in there. He's scared."

"But he's strong. He'll do fine."

Her heart kicked, and she closed her eyes

a moment. "He said he loved me." Her tears couldn't be restrained. They bubbled on her lids and then rolled down her cheeks.

Brent's expression softened. "Don't cry." He lifted his hand and swept away her tears. "I know Randy loves you."

"But . . ."

His eyes glazed with emotion. "Let him love you, Molly."

She searched his face.

"Because I love you, too."

Molly's breath jigged with each flutter of her heartbeat. She searched his eyes.

"You had to know." He brushed a few more stray tears from her cheek, his touch as light as butterfly wings.

"I hoped —" she saw the truth in his loving eyes "— but now I know for sure. I love you with all my heart."

A smile formed on his lips and charged to her heart. She wanted to kiss him, but she knew that would come later when they were alone. For now, she cherished the comfort of his arm around her shoulders and his hand in hers.

CHAPTER FIFTEEN

Molly left her office and headed to the back. The exciting but stressful past four weeks had taken their toll. She missed her time with Brent, and with school beginning soon, she felt torn.

Another woof resounded down the hallway. A new guest at the shelter hadn't adjusted yet. Her chest compressed as she headed toward the plaintive sounds. "What's wrong, Tilly?"

She scooted through the Dutch door and crouched beside the older cocker spaniel, its honey-colored coat needing more brushing. She cuddled the dog to her side, running her palm over its head and down its long silky ears. The neglected animal had been found in the apartment of an elderly woman who'd passed away.

When the dog had calmed, she placed him in the doggie bed and tossed him a rubber bone. He gave her a forlorn look and then nosed the bone and pawed at it. As his attention shifted from her to the toy, she inched open the door, slipped out and watched him for a moment before heading to the front.

Other than an occasional woof or whimper, the building remained quiet. Steph's doggie day care wouldn't move in until the beginning of September, another two weeks away, and with her opening, she'd acquired five dogs in the past week, but she knew more would come. So many more.

Now that summer had almost ended, Molly had begun advertising her Teacher's Pet program. She'd already spoken to a couple of her former students about volunteering with possible employment later, and she'd placed an ad for her obedience training classes in the local newspaper. For now, she needed to schedule her sessions after school hours.

Pleased with her progress thus far, she only regretted she'd had less time with Brent, who'd also been busy with a new project at work and caring for Randy. He'd finally have his cast off today.

Molly eyed her watch. Nearly dinnertime. She needed to let the dogs run outside for a short time, and then she would leave for the night, but not before turning on a radio.

She'd found the dogs liked the distraction. One day she'd like to hire someone to stay the night.

After locking the front door and placing the Closed sign in the window, Molly headed to the back and opened the doors of the pens. By the time she reached the side door, five eager tails were slapping against her legs. She eyed the outside fence to make sure it was locked and then opened the door. The five shot outside as if a starting gun signaled the beginning of a race.

She stood near the door, watching them scamper across the grass and head for the sandy area to relieve themselves, paw the dirt, then spring away, running in circles and chasing each other. Molly grinned at her perfect life and her answered prayer.

Tires crunched in the parking lot, and she turned to see Brent's sports car. Randy leaped from the passenger seat, his cast gone, and opened the back door. Rocket raced to the fence, his tail flailing like a whip. Molly waved and opened the gate to let Rocket inside. He flew across the grass and joined the frolicking pack. She watched to make sure it was an amiable welcome. It was.

Randy reached the gate first with Brent behind, an evasive look on his face. Since they'd opened their hearts to love, Molly had also opened her eyes. In the past three weeks when they were together, she'd studied every nuance of Brent's expression and behavior and had begun to read him well. Today he had something on his mind.

She kept her eyes on him as he approached.

"Look." Randy lifted his cast-free arm, his face flinching.

"Be careful. You have to watch that arm until it heals all the way."

"I know. The doctor told me."

She grinned. "What are you guys doing here?" She lifted her gaze again to Brent, still flashing his guilty look.

He slipped his arm around her shoulder. "We thought you might like to go out to dinner with us."

She peered at Randy's arm. "It's a celebration."

He chuckled. "Exactly."

"I think I can handle that." She motioned behind her. "I have to get them put up for the night."

"We'll help," Randy said, heading for the dogs.

Brent gave a whistle. "Not with that arm."

Randy spun around. So did the dogs. Randy scooted out of the way as the excited animals sprinted toward Brent, obviously responding to the whistle. Molly puckered her lips and failed. She needed to take whistling lessons.

She opened the door, and the dogs headed inside, even Rocket.

"Randy, you have something else to do. I'll help Molly." Brent gave him a knowing look and tilted his head toward the parking lot.

Randy's face burst into a smile, and he hustled to the car.

Though curious, she pushed her question aside and rounded up the dogs, putting them into their rooms, checking water dishes and closing the gated upper doors. Each dog she passed followed her with his eyes, making her feel as if she were abandoning them. "I'll see you guys in the morning."

Brent came down the hall with Rocket.

Molly had forgotten he'd come in with the others.

He stopped to attach his leash. "Ready?"

"Close. I need to do a couple things in the office."

"I'll put Rocket in the car."

She scooted past him and headed for her desk. Molly closed the computer windows and shut it down and then stacked her files.

When she looked up, Randy stood in front of her with a young dog cuddled in his left arm.

Molly melted. "You have another golden retriever?" She sailed to his side, and he settled the squirming dog in her arms. Its tongue lashed out and swept her across the cheek.

"He likes you."

"He likes you, too." The conversation sent her back to the one she had with Adam when she'd first met Brent. "What made you decide to get another dog?"

Brent stepped around Randy with a bag in his hand.

She eyed the sack and then the retriever.

He shook his head. "She's not mine."

Disbelief smacked her. "She's abandoned? How could anyone do that to this darling dog?" She looked down at the cuddly puppy, whose eyes followed her every movement.

Brent drew closer. "She was, but not anymore."

Her heart skipped. "What?"

"She's yours. A real teacher's pet."

Teacher's pet. Her eyes shifted from Brent to Randy, both wearing a ridiculous smile and both nodding yes.

"But . . . but I can't have a dog at the condo."

He slipped his arm around her shoulders. "We'll work something out."

Her mind spun. Work something out?

Randy grasped the paper bag from Brent's hand. "Here are her toys."

Toys? She felt Brent slip the dog from her arms while she stood there gaping at them and holding the sack.

Randy poked at it. "See what we bought her, Molly. Look inside."

Nothing made sense. Brent knew she wanted a dog one day, but her time wasn't her own right now . . . though he *was* a cute dog. But seeing Randy's eager face, she unwound the top and opened the bag. She tried to smile as she pulled out a ball, followed by a rawhide bone.

Brent and Randy stood beside her, their faces expectant and eyes focused on the sack. She delved in again and pulled out a box. Her mind reeled.

"Open it." Randy's eagerness spurred her on. Molly dropped the other items back into the sack and opened the box. Her pulse skipped in dizzy circles. A ring box. She looked at Brent, his smile growing while Randy bounced on his heels. "Come on. Open it."

She lifted out the black velvet case and raised the lid. A gorgeous diamond solitaire glinted at her, shooting red and blue rays. Her head inched upward, her eyes misting as the diamond's splendor blurred into a glistening prism.

"Ask her." Randy's whisper buzzed in her ears.

Brent clutched the dog tighter and knelt on the tile floor. "Molly, I'm asking you to be my wife, for better or worse, but I'm thinking better. I promise to love you always."

She clutched the diamond ring while joyful tears streamed down her cheeks. She gazed into two sets of amazing eyes, hearing laughter spring from her throat. "I wish I had a camera."

The dog gave Brent a wet swipe across the face, and he set her on the floor before he rose. The dog darted off with Randy following, and Molly greeted the moment alone to give Brent her answer. She tiptoed upward, curled her arms around his neck and gave him the longest, most precious kiss she'd ever given.

Brent drew her closer and kissed her again, filling her with overwhelming happiness.

"Would you mind if I name the dog Toby?"

He searched her face. "The dog's a girl.

Toby's a boy's name."

Molly gave him one of her determined looks. "Who says?"

Brent's serious expression broke into an amazing smile. "I love you, Molly."

"I love you."

Brent held her close, his lips brushing her cheek and nose, then settling on her lips.

Molly melted in his arms while three words bounced into her mind. *In God's time.* She needed to remember that. All good gifts came in God's time. Today she truly understood what that meant. She closed her eyes and sent a fervent thank-you to the Lord for His blessings.

A RECIPE FROM
GAIL GAYMER MARTIN

Many readers are curious about the dishes mentioned in some of my novels and want to try them. If you're one of those readers, here's my recipe for Chicken Paprikash and Spaetzel.

CHICKEN PAPRIKASH AND SPAETZEL

1 whole chicken cut in pieces or six chicken
  breasts
2 small onions sliced
2 Tbsp oil
2 Tbsp paprika
water to cover
salt to taste
4 pepperoncinis
1 16 oz container of sour cream
1/4 cup of flour
2 tsp of water

Brown onions in oil with paprika. Add chicken pieces, then cover with water. Add salt and pepperoncinis. Simmer until chicken is cooked (30 to 40 minutes). Remove chicken. To broth add sour cream which has 1/4 cup flour and water folded into it. Simmer for a few minutes until thick. Serve chicken on spaetzel noodles.

SPAETZEL

2 cups flour
2 eggs and 2 egg yolks
2/3 cup of milk
1 tbsp parley
1 1/2 tsp salt, pepper and nutmeg
1/4 cup butter and 1/2 cup breadcrumbs

Combine flour, eggs, milk and parsley. Place on cutting board and slide cherry-sized dollops into boiling water. Cook 5 minutes. Stir occasionally. Empty into colander and wash in cold water. ***When ready to serve, melt butter in pan, add spaetzel and crumbs and brown.

Dear Reader,

Pets are like family. They make us laugh, give us company and concern us when they are ill. We grieve when they die. I have wonderful memories of dogs and cats who touched my life through the years. Our daughter fostered and adopted dogs during her time on earth. She taught obedience training and participated in agility and fly-ball with her two border collies. Her love for dogs lives with us and inspired this novel. I hope you enjoyed Molly Manning's story as she worked to make her dream come true. We can accomplish wonderful things with the same drive and determination. Her love for the Lord was truly blessed, and her life was an example of faith for Brent and his father. If you love dogs as Molly did, you might want to learn more about Teacher's Pet at: www.teacherspet michigan.org and more about a "no more homeless pet community" at: www.oakland petfund.org. Your influence can make a difference in your neighborhood.

Look for the story of Molly's friend Steph in my next Love Inspired release. You will hear more from Molly and Brent, and maybe even go to their wedding.

Many blessings.
Gail Gaymen Martin

QUESTIONS FOR DISCUSSION

1. Two themes in this book are forgiveness and trust. How do these themes affect your life?

2. Molly's greatest struggle was to forgive herself. What kind of forgiveness is your greatest struggle?

3. Brent's lack of ability to trust was affected by his childhood. What kinds of trust issues affected Brent's life the most?

4. Molly promised herself to always be the best, never second best. What are the pros and cons of this goal?

5. Brent believed God had answered a prayer that caused his brother's tragedy. We know God hears our prayers. Discuss

prayer and how God hears and answers them.

6. Brent's father told him that he'd made a lot of mistakes raising his family, and now he didn't know how to fix it. Brent said, "You've just started." What does Brent mean, and what changes have been made to repair their relationship? What does this mean to your life?

7. Through much of the novel, Brent could not forgive himself for his past. How does I John 3:19–20, the Bible verses theme, relate to him? *We will be confident when we stand before the Lord, even if our hearts condemn us. For God is greater than our hearts, and He knows everything.*

8. Of these four characters — Morris, Brent, Molly, Steph — who relates to you most and why?

9. Dogs are an important part of this novel. What lessons can we learn from our pets?

10. Molly identified "spiritual" lessons people can learn from their dogs. What are some of these lessons she mentioned?

Have you learned a spiritual lesson from your pet?

11. What do pets, especially dogs, mean to you and your family? Explain why you have or haven't owned a pet.

12. Molly felt strongly about protecting dogs and providing them a good home. What is your view on this issue? What is your attitude toward euthanasia?

ABOUT THE AUTHOR

Gail Gaymer Martin is a multi-award-winning author published in fiction and nonfiction. Her novels have received numerous national awards, and she has over two and a half million books in print. She writes women's fiction, romance and romantic suspense for Steeple Hill Books and Barbour Publishing and is the author of *Writing the Christian Romance* from Writer's Digest Books. Gail is a cofounder of American Christian Fiction Writers.

When not behind her computer, she enjoys a busy life — traveling, presenting workshops at conferences, speaking at churches and libraries, and singing as a soloist and member of her church choir, where she also plays handbells and handchimes. She also sings with one of the finest Christian chorales in Michigan, the Detroit Lutheran Singers. Gail lives in Michigan with her husband, Bob. To learn more about her, visit her Web site at www.gailmartin.com. Write to Gail at P.O. Box 760063, Lathrup Village, MI 48076, or at authorgailmartin@aol.com. She enjoys hearing from readers.

We hope you have enjoyed this Large Print book. Other Thorndike, Wheeler, Kennebec, and Chivers Press Large Print books are available at your library or directly from the publishers.

For information about current and upcoming titles, please call or write, without obligation, to:

Publisher
Thorndike Press
295 Kennedy Memorial Drive
Waterville, ME 04901
Tel. (800) 223-1244

or visit our Web site at:

http://gale.cengage.com/thorndike

OR

Chivers Large Print
published by BBC Audiobooks Ltd
St James House, The Square
Lower Bristol Road
Bath BA2 3SB
England
Tel. +44(0) 800 136919
email: bbcaudiobooks@bbc.co.uk
www.bbcaudiobooks.co.uk

All our Large Print titles are designed for easy reading, and all our books are made to last.